Eagle Flight

Eagle Flight

Ken Wilbur

authorHOUSE®

AuthorHouse™
1663 Liberty Drive
Bloomington, IN 47403
www.authorhouse.com
Phone: 1 (800) 839-8640

Published by AuthorHouse 07/24/2015

ISBN: 978-1-5049-2565-5 (sc)
ISBN: 978-1-5049-2564-8 (e)

Print information available on the last page.

Any people depicted in stock imagery provided by Thinkstock are models, and such images are being used for illustrative purposes only.
Certain stock imagery © Thinkstock.

This book is printed on acid-free paper.

Because of the dynamic nature of the Internet, any web addresses or links contained in this book may have changed since publication and may no longer be valid. The views expressed in this work are solely those of the author and do not necessarily reflect the views of the publisher, and the publisher hereby disclaims any responsibility for them.

Ken Wilbur

I owe so many thanks but especially to: Herman Hoepfner, Art Schlee, Junior Bronn and Dale Wolf. I can never repay them for all they did for me.

A special thanks to my sister Ardath for proof reading and putting up with my love for the comma. I also wish to thank my daughter Angee for her photography work and her daughter Sarah for her modeling.

DEDICATION

I would like to dedicate this novel to Randalia, Iowa. My Dear Lord could not have picked a better place for me to grow up. Randalia, located in Fayette County in northeast Iowa was small but the people were so awesome. Billy Johnson, Duane Schroeder, Jerry Cue and myself roamed the streets and every back alley. We played ball behind the church and when we really got hold of one we would break a window in Mary and Earl's house. But Earl had the hardware store so he fixed it and we continued to play.

My high school graduating class: Elvin Nading, President, Duane Schroeder, Vice-president, Rita Smith, Secretary and her twin brother Rial was treasurer. Bill Hanson, Harold Schlatter, Roene Burghardt, Clifford Vierow, Jerry Cue, Sharon Butts, Harry Drews, Laverne Wolfgram, and I had a class motto: "Push, Pull, or get out of the way." Vernon McFadden and Kenny Miner were a grade behind us but they were very much a part of our success. We dedicated our senior annual to our good friend custodian George Carley who would open the gym for us to shoot baskets and helped us with special projects.

CHAPTER ONE

She thumbed back the hammer of her Remington .41 caliber derringer. With the muzzle pressed against his head just behind the ear, she leaned over and spoke with a soft but angry tone of voice.

"We have been in St. Louis a week, getting nothing but the run around. I want some answers and if I don't get them I hope you told your wife and kids good bye this morning." She was petite but not weak. She did not look to be as strong as she was. She had waited five years to get some answers about the death of her father and her patience was wearing thin.

"James, look in that file cabinet and see if you can find anything." James was tall, six-two, a hundred and ninety pounds. Broad shoulders, a thick chest with a small waist. His arms showed the signs of the hard work he had done in the past.

"Mr. Collins, my father had your name circled in the papers we got out of his lockbox. Tell me what you know of his death."

"It could have been anyone of a number of people. There were over a hundred convictions, many more were indicted. I admit I took money to kill my story, but that is all that I did." His voice showed of the fear he felt. He was not a strong man that is why he took the money in exchange for his silence.

"Denise, I've got a large file here on the Whiskey Ring." James pulled a thick folder from the cabinet.

"Yes, that is all my notes, it will tell you how the scandal worked, all the payoffs but it won't shed any light on the death of your father. All I can tell you is that because of your father the ring was broken up. His death triggered the federal agents to seize control of over sixteen distilleries and place several Internal Revenue Offices under control of the Treasury Department."

"Where is my father's grave?"

"Jefferson Barracks National Cemetery on Sheridan Road."

"Now, wouldn't it have been much easier for you to just tell me these things when I first asked?" She took the Remington from behind his ear and slowly released the hammer.

"You don't understand, this Whiskey Ring was bigger than anyone knows and even after five years you are in great danger asking questions. I didn't tell you anything because I didn't want you to end up like your father."

"You think I should just walk away?"

"I think you should go visit your father's grave. I think you should regale in all that your father accomplished. You know far better than I what your father would want you to do. I would suggest that you go see Sgt. Bob Miner at the Second Police substation at 220 Chestnut, Bob is one of the good guys."

James handed Denise the folder and closed the file cabinet.

"You can take those notes, read them and you will have a better idea of what your father was up against. I would strongly suggest that you tell no one you have those notes."

"Why?"

"Because they could get you killed. There are still a great number of people in St. Louis who do not want them made public."

"As soon as we leave are you going to call the police and tell them we came in here with a gun and stole these papers?"

"No, I owe your father more than that." He paused. "Your father was a good man, he helped me greatly. Be careful who you talk to and who you ask questions. People are like books, you can never tell by the cover what's inside. Like a good book they can surprise you."

CHAPTER TWO

"Sister Denise, please come in." Father Heilman was not the picture you may have of a priest. He was tall, square shouldered, blond headed and spoke with a slight German accent.

"Now may I help you Sister Denise?"

"Today is my birthday, I am twenty." Her voice was hesitant, undecided.

"Have you made a decision?"

"Yes, I have to go and find out what I can about my father. I made a promise to him to do nothing until my twentieth birthday."

"Very well." Father Heilman paused as he reached for a pad on his big oak desk. "I will release you from your vows Sister Denise. I want you to know you are always welcome to come back at any time. The students will miss you."

"Do you wish for me to stay until you can get a replacement?"

"No, we will manage. I think being you have made the decision to go, that it is best that you not tarry."

Denise still had her old clothes. They had been loose and baggy five years ago, now they were too tight for her more mature body. She would have to buy some new things.

She still had the things her father had helped her sew into the lining of her jacket. She cut it open to find several two dollar bills, a twenty and two fifty dollar bills. There was also a key to a lock box at the First National Bank of Saint Louis.

She would have money to buy some new clothes and make the trip but she would have to be frugal. That had never been a problem for her in the past and so she didn't feel that it would be now. If anything the last five years would help her to avoid unnecessary spending.

At the store she tried on a dress with a narrow skirt that the lady had told her was the latest style. It made walking difficult and it was not even that comfortable to sit in. She did not want anything exuberant with a bunch of trim and frill. She found a green print calico dress that was comfortable. A white pinafore that she could wear over it to make it look like two different outfits was added to her pile. She liked a tan duster that would protect her clothes from dust, rain and soot. It had a nice deep pocket where she could carry her little Remington.

She would also have to buy some things to take to eat on the train. She remembered the rancid meat, cold beans and old coffee at the places where the train stopped to get water. The food in the dining car was good, but expensive, a bowl of soup was forty cents and a meal cost a dollar fifty plus tip.

She still had to purchase her ticket and say good bye. She didn't look forward to saying good bye and explaining why she was doing what she planned to do. She knew she would never be able to put her heart and soul into anything until she went back to St. Louis and made an attempt to find out what happened to her father.

Her mother died when she was very young, her father who was a federal agent raised her. He taught her to ride and shoot. The Whiskey Ring case he was investigating in St. Louis for the Secretary of Treasury was especially dangerous. He had given her instructions what to do if for some reason he did not return to their hotel room. She was to go to the convent and lie about her age. He told her what to say and what not to say. He made her promise to stay until she was twenty. At that time she could remain or go back to public life, it was her decision to make.

As she walked out into the court yard for what could be the last time, she looked up into the sky to see an eagle soaring in the thermal currents high overhead. She wondered what it would feel like to be so free, so powerful. Was she, like the eagle, taking flight or was she fleeing, running away?

CHAPTER THREE

James was watching an eagle on an old dead Ponderosa Pine high up on the south rim of the canyon.

"Wade spoke to me of your problem James." James turned to see his father. "You will never be truly happy until you chase this dream. You will continue to struggle with this until you go and find your way."

"Sometimes father the pain and emotions explode inside of me."

"You do not need my approval. Have a heart-to-heart talk with God. Your Lord may have a plan for you outside Eagle Valley but your mother and I want you to know you are always welcome to come back."

"I have prayed about this. I will continue to pray to do the right thing."

"Remember James, the devil always dresses up evil and makes it look good." Jokob put his hand on his son's shoulder. It was not the Amish way to show love and affection. Jokob and his family had long ago broken away from the Amish church, but he still held to his upbringing.

"Thank you, father." James looked up to see the eagle take flight from the limb. He too was about to take flight from Eagle Valley.

It did not take him long to pack his things and say good bye, he did not even know where he was going or what he would do. He would start in Golden City. He had thought about going to school at the Colorado School of Mines or get a job at the paper mill or flour mill.

He had saved a little money but he knew it would not last long if he had to rent a room and buy his meals. He was riding down 12th Street in Golden City when he saw this girl come out of a dry goods store. She was wearing a blue calico dress with a matching bonnet but when James saw her eyes he knew she was the girl he had seen as a nun. He watched as she walked to the train station. He dismounted, and followed her into the depot. He watched as she walked up to the counter and purchased a ticket. Her bonnet hid her face but he saw her eyes again when she turned to leave. It was the same girl.

"I would like a ticket just like the one that girl just got."

The ticket agent looked at James with a smile of understanding. "A second class ticket to St. Louis is eighteen dollars and seventy cents."

That was almost all the money James had but if she was going to St. Louis he could not stay in Golden City. He counted out the money and the agent gave him his ticket. He looked at it hoping to see a day and time but there was none. He looked up at a big board that said the next train going east would be at six pm. The big clock next to the board said it was almost two.

He got his horse and rode to the stable just a little more than a block away. He would sell his horse and saddle. That would give him a little money.

"I can't buy your horse, got more than I need." The hostler turned and took a seat on a feed sack. He spit tobacco juice at a bug crawling on the dirt floor at his feet. Brown colored saliva ran from the corner of his mouth staining his silver whiskers.

"You know anyone that might be interested in buying a good horse?"

"You could try the Holmes brothers down on Washington Avenue, they trade horses." He pointed with a bony finger toward the street.

James had better luck with the Holmes brothers but they knew they had the advantage, so he got only about half of what the horse and tack were worth. He took his saddle bags and the fifty dollars and headed for the general store. He wanted to get some jerky, dried apples, a loaf of bread, and a glazed stoneware jug of apple cider to take on the train. He had never been on a train but he had heard stories that food was expensive.

He wished he could let his family know he was taking this trip to St. Louis but he couldn't think of a way to do that. The only thing he could think of was to go to the post office and leave a letter addressed to his father, hoping he would come and ask if there was any mail for him. He wrote a short note asking them not to worry that he was going by train to St. Louis.

He went to the depot to wait and see if the girl got on the six o'clock train. He knew he was looking at this through rose-colored glasses but it was not a time that he could be practical. If he used the good sense he was born with, he would still be in the valley watching the eagles and wishing he were elsewhere.

CHAPTER FOUR

"Are you following me?" Denise asked as James took the seat next to her on the train.

"Ah, no I am not following you." He looked down at his feet, he had thought of what to say while waiting in the station. At the moment nothing came to mind.

"You are the same young man that came to the mission school."

"Yes, that was me."

With a lunge the train pulled out of the station. The lowest price ticket, third class, would have them in an open car with wooden bench seats. One washroom to be shared by both men and women. Very often unsavory company to get to it. Their level, second class, had an enclosed passenger car with padded seats. A men and ladies washroom at opposite ends of the car. The first class passengers enjoyed the Pullman sleeping car. It had leather upholstered seats that folded down into beds. Curtains that closed for privacy and porters to attend passenger's needs.

The railroad made travel faster, less difficult and more economical than the wagon train or stage lines. The small wood burning locomotives capable of pulling a dozen or so cars had been replaced with the larger coal burning locomotives that could handle more cars at a greater speed. With the competition of the two lines, prices had dropped from over a hundred dollars for a ticket from Denver to St. Louis to twenty-five for a first class ticket.

It did not take the train long to get up to speed, it was a gradual downhill run from the mile high altitude in Colorado to the flat lands of Kansas. The train would reach speeds up to thirty-five miles per hour.

"If you are not following me where at you going?"

"I have a ticket to St. Louis."

"What will you do in St. Louis?"

James was at a loss for words. He did not even know himself why he was going to St. Louis, how could he hope to explain it to her. He was about to do his best to attempt to explain his positon when he was interrupted.

Two young men in seats across the aisle had been sharing a jug of moonshine of sorts. They now had some liquid courage to act on what they had been thinking.

"What's a pretty bonny lass like you doing with this wanker?" They stood in the aisle leaning over to talk to Denise. She started to turn and rise, but James's hand on her arm made her hesitate long enough for him to act. With a short but very violent upper cut to the first man's solar plexus of his upper abdomen and reaching around to grab the second man behind the head and smash his face into the head of the first man, the fight was over before it even got a good start. The first man was in great pain with difficulty in breathing as he had the wind knocked out of him. The second man's nose was broken and blood was pouring out all over him and the back of the first man.

James gave them a push and they both staggered back to their seats. The short but explosive encounter had gone unnoticed for the most part. The one gentlemen and his traveling companion that did witness it seemed to enjoy the outcome by the looks of approval on their faces.

"I am going to have to get a new hat and a different jacket, what I am wearing tends to send the wrong message to some folks."

"It also tends to make them under estimate you. Think it worked to your advantage this time."

It was dark and James pulled his hat down over his eyes and leaned back and went to sleep. The rocking of the train and the sound of the steel wheels on the iron rails soon had him sound asleep.

James awoke to the sound of a child crying. Earlier he had seen a mother and small boy, three years of age or younger board the train. James noted that they had no bags of any kind with them but didn't think much of it.

"Mommy, I am hungry." The people around them were eating breakfast they had either purchased in the snack car or brought with them on the train.

The mother was doing her best to explain something to the small boy but he wasn't buying any of it. He was hungry and he wanted something to eat.

James got to his feet and checked his pocket for change. He had seen his father do this for years and he had practiced in his room but had never done it. He was blessed with large hands, long slender fingers and good dexterity. He was about to see if he could put them to good use.

"Good morning young man," James spoke to the youngster as he approached their seats. "Let's see what we have here?" He touched the boy's ear and it produced a nickel. He handed it to the lad who looked up at him with big blue eyes of bewilderment.

James touched his other ear and it too produced a nickel. He dropped it into the boy's hand. Cupping the boy's nose with his right hand nickels fell out of it into his left hand. Three more nickels, he dropped into the boy's waiting hand.

"You just have nickels hiding everywhere," he said with a big smile as he rubbed the boy's head.

"Thank you, Oh thank you so much." James nodded to the woman and returned to his seat.

"Where did you learn that?"

"My father, he is very good at sleight of hand tricks. He does them to show that everything is not always as it seems."

"Looks like you have some of his talent. That was a nice way to help them." Denise was wrapped in a small blanket, her bonnet had worked forward and almost hide her eyes from view.

"Are you sorry that you came on the train?"

"No, I am where I need to be in order to get to where I want to be."

"And where pray tell is that?"

"I just want to enjoy the journey, I will worry about the destination later."

Denise and James walked out of the Union Depot in St. Louis to heavy rain. Even with the rain pouring down they could smell the pollution in the air. Coal dust and smoke hung in the air like a cap over the city. They had heard that they could get a nice boarding house for twelve dollars a week, board and room. They had no idea where to go.

"Hello! May we give you a lift?" They looked up to see a fancy rig, all enclosed pulled by a matching pair of gray horses with black mane and tail. They did not recognize the man leaning out of the door. They were about to say, "No thanks." When they saw the little boy from the train.

It was crowded with all of them and their bags but it was much better than walking in the rain.

"Where could we drop you? But first I want to thank you for helping my wife and son on the train. That was very nice of you."

"You are welcome. We don't know, we have heard that there are some nice boarding houses that are not too expensive."

"Yes, I know of just the one if she has room. Clarence, take us to Siefken's boarding house on Fourth Street. Nice German lady, the place is clean and she is an excellent cook."

"Can you pull another nickel out of my ear?" The little boy was holding his ear lobe and looking at James with big eyes of hope.

Lucky for James they pulled up in front of the boarding house. "Clarence, please step inside and see if Mrs. Siefken has a room."

"We need two rooms, please."

Mrs. Siefken was widowed with a large home and no income. So she turned her home into a boarding house. It cost twelve dollars a week with two meals, breakfast at seven sharp and dinner at six. A bell was rung when the food was ready, it was family style, first come first served. You were on time if you wanted to eat, no exceptions.

"Why do you eat with your fork in your left hand?" Jesse was Mrs. Siefken's nephew, a nice young man if not the brightest star in the sky.

Mr. Hutching's the only English gentleman at the table who always dressed for meals and had very excellent table manners put down his fork and wiped his mouth with his napkin.

"That reminds me of the American that boarded a train to London and could not find a place to rest. He walked the whole train looking for an empty seat. The only unoccupied seat was directly adjacent to a well-dressed middle aged lady and was being used by her little dog.

The weary American asked, "Please, Ma'am, may I sit in that seat?"

The English woman looked down her nose at him, sniffed and said, "You Americans. You are such a rude class of people. Can't you see my little Fife is using that seat?"

Again he walked the train and found nothing until he found himself facing the woman again. "Please, lady. May I sit there? I am tired." The English woman wrinkled her nose and snorted, "You Americans! Not only are you rude, you are also arrogant."

He didn't say anything, he leaned over picked up the little dog, tossed it out the window of the train and sat down in the empty seat.

An English gentleman sitting across the aisle spoke up. "You Americans do seem to have a penchant for doing the wrong thing. You eat holding the fork in the wrong hand and now sir you're thrown the wrong bitch out the window." They all laughed even old Mrs. Bender who saw very little humor in anything.

"It saves time my lad. You cut your meat, lay down your knife and pick up your fork to eat. I cut my meat with my knife in my right hand my fork in my left. I continue to eat and cut, where as you continue to lay down your knife and pick up your fork."

They were enjoying Wiener Schnitzel but because veal was too expensive, Mrs. Siefken had made it out of pork that she had pounded. They had German potato salad, sweet corn, a hot roll and hot tea or coffee. For dessert she had made plum pudding.

James looked around the table and could not believe the changes in his life in just the last few days. He had to admit that things were going well, he hoped their good luck continued.

CHAPTER FIVE

Sgt. Miner was a big man, over six feet and two hundred pounds. His dark hair was turning silver at the temples, and getting a little thin on top. In his large hands he was holding a little black and white puppy.

"You wouldn't be in need of a little pup would you? Picked him up down near the river. Think he could be a witness to a crime that was committed last night but don't think the judge will let him testify."

"No, sir. I am Denise Fisher, my father was John Fisher. Mr. Collins at the Globe told us that maybe you could help us."

"What is it that you would like help with?"

"Well, a police report on my father's death. His belongings. The only thing we have been able to learn was the little that was in the newspaper."

"John Fisher? When was his death?"

"He was killed May tenth, 1875."

Sgt. Miner got to his feet and took a box off a shelf behind his desk. He removed the works of an old wooden clock. Gears, wheels, and springs that years ago had been a working time piece. He dumped them into a desk drawer and placed the little puppy in the box. He closed the lid, leaving a crack so the pup could get air.

"We will have to go down in the basement and see if we have anything that was five years ago."

"Yes, my father was sent to St. Louis by Benjamin Bristow, he was to investigate the siphoning off of federal liquor taxes." Denise and James followed Sgt. Miner out of his office and down a hall to a door leading to the basement. As they descended the stairs the smell of damp and moldy paper filled the air.

"Everything should be labeled by month and year. May 1875 should be down here on the top shelf." Sgt. Miner carried the coal oil lantern high in his left hand. "Things are not always where they should be however."

After a short search, they found what they were looking for. "Let's take this to my office where we can see well." Sgt. Miner carried the wooden crate up the stairs to his office. Denise and James followed.

"Let's see what we have here?"

Her father's revolver, a Modele, double action revolver with an octagonal barrel. Sgt. Miner showed Denise and James that there were two spent cartridges in it.

"My father always carried it with a spent cartridge under the hammer, but never two."

"That could mean that he fired it just before his death."

Sgt. Miner handed her a tintype, it was a picture of a man and a young girl.

"We had this taken at the ball park just a few days before his death. We went to watch the Red Stockings play a team from Chicago."

A wallet with an identification card showed John Fisher to be a federal agent. There was no money but it did contain a folded piece of paper. Denise unfolded it. "I cannot prepare a path for you, I hope I have prepared you for the path."

CHAPTER SIX

Denise and James were high above the Mis-sis-sip coming from the north and the Mis-sou-rah branching in from the west. They could see the eagles in the trees on the granite bluffs overlooking the rivers. The eagles would take flight to soar above the water then dive to the surface of the river to grab a fish.

They had just come from lunch at a bar full of nooks and crannies with tables and booths and the best food on the river. It was old and rustic but clean and comfortable. They were waiting to see if Sgt. Miner had been able to find out if anyone had been admitted to the hospital on May 10th or 11th with a gunshot wound.

Sgt. Miner was on horse patrol today and he told them he would meet them here after lunch. He did not think it was a good idea for them to come to the station. He suspected there were some officers that had taken bribes that were still on the force and did not want to be found out.

They heard the horse shoes on the street before they saw him round the corner of the building. He was riding a big bay gelding, but he made the horse look small. For such a large man he sat the saddle well. He did not dismount as he did not want anyone that may be watching to think he knew the couple. It appeared from a distance that a police officer was just speaking to a couple who were watching the eagles.

"Three men were admitted, one at eleven pm on the 10th and two more early in the morning on the 11th. One is dead, one is in prison and the other was a player on the Chicago White Stockings baseball team. George Red Foster." Sgt. Miner swung his arm in a half circle and pointed" toward the south as if he were giving directions or telling them about the area. He put his heel to the bay and turning rode on up the river.

"That could be why your father was at the baseball game. He could have been following a lead and wanted to see this Foster."

"In the notes that Mr. Collins gave us it said the Whisky Ring started in Chicago. Who would suspect a baseball player if he were sent to St. Louis to silence my father?"

"That was five years ago. We need to go to the park and check the schedule and see if this Foster is still playing for Chicago."

They learned that the 1877 St. Louis team was embroiled in a game-fixing scandal and kicked out of the league. They were just now starting to play out of town teams again but were still not part of the league. So the Chicago team would not be coming to St. Louis. They could not find out anything about Foster.

Going back over the notes of Collins they found one common denominator. In many of the major cities, the Whiskey Ring and the baseball team were controlled by the same people the beer breweries and the distilleries. The owners tended to do anything to win. In 1879 the owners had put in a reserve clause, each National League team was allowed to "reserve" five players for the next season. These players could not be enticed to play for any other National League team.

They also learned that the 1875 St. Louis team won only four games the whole season. The next year the 1876 team record was 45 wins and 19 losses, a huge turn around. That could explain why the 1877 team was kicked out of the league.

"It seems like we have run into a dead end here in St. Louis." James turned his attention back to the eagles fishing below the dam in the Mississippi River. Some of the fish going over the dam would be stunned, knocked unconscious. These were easy prey for the eagles.

"Yes. I wish we could learn more about Foster. I wonder if Mr. Collins could help us with that. I would like to return his notes and thank him for pointing us to Sgt. Miner."

"It may be best for him if we don't go back to the newspaper. We could go to his home."

It seemed natural for them to work as a pair. Neither knew when it first became comfortable for them, it just seemed to happen. They were a team but either of them talked about it. James tended to follow her lead but she would often ask his advice. They were both learning as they were living, and both hoping for a good tomorrow.

CHAPTER SEVEN

Mrs. Siefken had made them some blueberry streusel muffins and packed them a lunch to take on the train. They learned that Red Foster was now the player/manager for the Chicago White Stockings. They played their home games at Lake Front Park and were enjoying a home stand for the next six games.

James noticed a man watching them, he looked like the same man he had seen in the train station in St. Louis that was paying them more than normal attention. He looked like any number of men on the train. He was average height, average weight, in his late thirties. His shirt was the only thing that was a little different about him. It was a well-tailored navy flannel with two pockets. A large pocket over his heart and a small pocket on his right. James would remember the shirt if not the man.

Their train pulled into the Randolph Street Station on Michigan Avenue. The station was within blocks of the Lake Front Park and several hotels up Michigan Avenue.

"Let's see if we can find a hotel before we do anything." James gathered up their bags and stepped back into the aisle to allow Denise to go ahead of him.

The first hotel they came to was the Kirkwood. They did not see the doorman frown as he opened the door for them. They stepped into the lobby to find a courthouse type atmosphere. Hallways and floors lined with marble. Several large chandeliers lighted the room filled with black leather overstuffed chairs.

"This could be a little more than we need or can afford." Denise turned to look at James who nodded in agreement.

As they went out one door, James noticed the man from the train go in the other door. It could be just chance, accidental, but James did think so.

The next hotel, the Brown, looked clean and more like what they were looking for. The lobby was not so large, not so elaborate. The marble floors not so shiny and the chairs looked comfortable but not as expensive as those in the Kirkwood.

They got rooms with a wash room for two dollars a night. They paid for just one night as they did not know how long they would be in Chicago. They hoped to talk to this Foster, find out what he knew and how he got shot. They put their things in their rooms and went to find Foster.

It was not a long walk to the Lake Front Park, home of the Chicago White Stocking. It was just a couple blocks north and a couple blocks east of the hotel. It was mid-morning and the team had a game that afternoon so Red Foster should be at the park.

The wind was out of the southwest and it carried with it the smoke and smell from the many factories and forges in south Chicago. At times they could smell the Chicago Stock yards which was an improvement over the factories and forges.

The police officer at the gate to the park would not allow them to enter. He told them the player's entrance was around the corner, they could try their luck there. The police officer here was checking passes.

"You got to have a press pass or a player's pass." The big Irish cop seemed to have a permanent smile on his face but was not going to allow them to enter.

"We would like to speak with Mr. Foster."

"You and a hundred other fans, but that's not going to happen." He gave them the bad news with a big Irish smile and a twinkle in his eyes.

It cost fifty cents to see the game, but they would not allow fans to enter for another hour or longer. They had time to walk around and see if they could learn anything of value. They came to Wabash Ave.

and turned back south. After a block or two, they came to Belford &
Clark Publishers. As they stood and looked in the window at some
of their publications, Denise got an idea.

"Wait for me, I will only be a minute."

Inside she could smell the print and paper. The room had a desk and
several chairs. A small man, with a thin mustache and an eye shade
sat behind the scarred oak desk. He looked up at Denise but said
nothing.

"Are you hiring?"

"What job you want? What can you do?"

"Writing, or art work would be my first choices."

The man looked her up and down, as if reading her resume. He
slowly got to his feet, "Give me a minute, be right back." He turned
and disappeared behind a partition. Denise noticed on the desk a
stack of letterhead stationary with Belford & Clark on it, also some
business cards. She took one of each and put them behind her purse
next to her body. As she stepped back the man appeared with a sheet
of paper in his hand.

"Take this, bring it back when you got it all filled out. We have not
hired any women in the past but Mr. Clark thinks maybe we should."

"Thank you, I appreciate this opportunity." Denise took the paper
and turned to leave.

As they walked, Denise told James of what had transpired and what
she did.

"For a nun you are very devious."

"Ex-nun."

"What do you plan to do with them?"

"Not sure. I thought maybe I could get Foster to think Belford & Clark were going to do a story about him. I think we should go watch the ball game, get an idea of what Foster does and what he looks like. I would like to go back to my room and drop these off before we go to the game."

At the game, they learned how Foster got his nickname. He wore a sporty red handlebar mustache that made him easy to spot on the field. If not the best, he was one of the best on the team. He played first base and hit third in the Chicago line up.

The team was having a great year, the fans were happy and most of their home games were near capacity. The park had a grandstand that held two thousand fans at a dollar a seat. The bleachers held six thousand at fifty cents a seat and the eighteen luxury boxes on the third base line held a hundred at five dollars a seat. These luxury box seats were armchairs with curtains for privacy.

James and Denise had seats near first base in the bleachers. The Chicago team had the third base dugout so they could watch Foster on and off the field. The park being right downtown, where land was such a premium, was small. A ball hit out of the park to right field landed on the railroad tracks. If the wind was blowing out it could land in Lake Michigan. It was only 200 feet to the right field fence so it was ruled a ground rule double.

The umpire standing about fifteen feet to the batter's side was wearing a bowler hat and smoking a cigar. The hurler waited until the umpire called, "Striker to the line," to make his pitch to the catcher. Three strikes and the batter was out but it took seven balls for him to be awarded a walk. A foul ball was not a strike, it was called a no pitch. But any foul tip caught by the catcher regardless of the number of strikes on the batter and he was out.

The catcher had a mask and chest protector but no chin guards. He had a fingerless glove on both hands and caught the ball with both hands. He sat several feet behind the batter so that most of the low pitches bounced before they got to him.

Foster playing first base wore a fingerless glove. The glove covered the palm of his hand and the first knuckle of his fingers. It had no laces between the thumb and first finger. It looked like an improvised work glove but had been made by a saddle maker out of saddle leather.

There was a box outlined in chalk for the pitcher. It was six feet deep and four feet wide. The front of the box was fifty feet from home plate. The hurler had to begin each pitch and end each pitch inside this box.

They listened to the fans as much as they watched the game. They learned that Foster was very popular and by many considered the best player on the team.

After the game, James and Denise went around to the player's entrance to watch and see what happened. After about thirty minutes the players began to exit. Fans were waiting to get an autograph and some of the more popular players had a difficult time getting to a waiting surrey.

After about an hour, the fans began to dissipate. It was not long and there was only one carriage and James and Denise were the only fans still waiting.

Red Foster was wearing a long gray suit coat almost to his knees, black straight leg trousers, a white shirt and purple vest. The spats covering his shoes matched his vest. His red hair was parted down the middle and slicked back. But it was the diamond stick pin in his black tie that caught their eye.

They watched him walk to the carriage and start up the street. They walked as fast as they could to watch where he was going. But it was not long and the carriage was out of sight. They made their way north to Randolph St. as this was the last they saw of Foster's surrey.

They saw the carriage in front of The Store. The Store owned by Mike McDonald was a saloon on the first floor, a casino on the second and a flop house on the third and fourth. It was said in Chicago that it was McDonald and not P.T. Barnum who coined the phrase, "There is a sucker born every minute." It was also said if you did anything shady in Chicago and did not have his blessing, you were in real trouble. This was also the start of what was called Hair-trigger Block. Named that because there were shootings almost every night. So long as the shootings were confined to Hair-trigger Block, the police did not intervene.

Dime novels romanticized the numerous cow towns of Kansas. Wichita, Abilene and Dodge City along with Deadwood and Tombstone Arizona. But the truth was, there were more gun fights in Hair-trigger Block than in all these famous cow towns added together.

CHAPTER EIGHT

"They write about me and the team every day in the three papers, why would Belford and Clark want to add to this?" Red Foster was about half dressed for the game. He was wearing his baseball pants and an undershirt that he wore under his jersey.

"This would be different. The Times, Tribune, and Daily News write about the on field Red Foster. We want to write more in depth about your wants, dreams, and desires." Denise took the letter of introduction from him and put it under the notebook she held in her hands.

"When ya want to do this?" There was a knock on the door. "Yeah, whata ya want?"

"Any change in today's line up?"

"No, post the one I gave you?" Red reached for his game jersey hanging in a locker.

"Whenever it is convenient for you. Our first interview shouldn't take more than a half hour." Denise wrote something on her note pad waiting for his reply.

"Well, let's try it today after the game. Give us about forty-five minutes and come to the gate. I will tell Clancy to let you in." He was buttoning his jersey as he spoke.

"Great, and thank you Mr. Foster, this is going to be very special." He pointed to the door to the outside as he turned to go out the other door.

James could tell by the smile on her face that it had gone well. They had talked at length about what was the best way to approach Foster.

They wanted him to feel special, comfortable. The last thing they wanted was for him to get defensive.

"I am to have an interview today after the game. It went well, just as we hoped it would." She had a bounce, a skip in her step like a young school girl that was happy with herself.

"I am starting to get low on money. I thought of going to the stock yards to see about getting a job. Guess I can wait until tomorrow morning to see how this goes. You may learn something."

"Let's take a walk down to the lake. I want to make a list of questions to ask Foster without making him suspect anything." It was only a couple blocks around the ball park to the lake shore. As they walked past the ticket window James saw the man that had followed them from St. Louis. He was wearing a different shirt but James was sure it was the same man. He was talking to one of the venders that sold programs outside the park.

A slight breeze was blowing in off the lake bringing with it the smell of fish and water. They could see several small fishing boats not far from shore. On the beach were several families enjoying the sun and water. They found a large rock off to one side where they could relax and talk about how to get the most out of the interview.

They could hear the crowd at the ball park erupt with a roar from time to time when the home team did something that pleased them. The afternoon pasted quickly and it was soon time for them to head back to the ball park.

"Come in Ms. Fisher, have a seat." Foster was still in uniform. A uniform covered with dirt and wet with sweat.

"Thank you, I appreciate you doing this. I hope we can come up with something that you are pleased with." She took her seat and got her notebook ready to take notes.

"Why don't you go to the door and wave for your friend to come in and join us." Foster got up and went to the other door, opened it and stepped aside to allow a man to enter.

James stepped into the manager's office to come face to face with the man from St. Louis. Denise standing just inside the door slide her hand into her purse to grip the Remington.

"This is Paul Wheeler, I'm Red Foster, I don't think we have meant." He extended his hand to James. "Why don't you both sit down and tell us what you know?"

James did not acknowledge Foster's hand. His eyes were locked on those of Wheeler.

"I don't understand, I thought this was going to be an interview." Denise was still standing, feeling very uncomfortable.

"You don't think that you fooled us with that fake letter and wanting to do a story about me do you? Now, please have a seat and tell us what you have learned." He motioned with his palm up toward the chairs on their side of the oak desk. "We know that you talked to Mr. Collins in St. Louis. We know that you went to see Sgt. Miner and got your father's things. Did you learn anything else and have you passed any information on to anyone?"

"We learned that you were shot the same night my father was killed."
"Ms. Fisher, I was with your father the night he was killed in St. Louis. I was working undercover for Mr. Bristow. I am now working with Mr. Wheeler. We cannot have you nosing around and messing up our investigation."

Denise looked from Foster to Wheeler and then to James. Rejected she slipped into the chair. This was not what she had expected, she was at a loss for words.

"Mr. Wheeler had gone to St. Louis to follow up on a couple of leads but they turned out to be dead ends when he ran into you two." Foster took a seat behind his desk. "Your father shot and killed the man that killed him and wounded me. He was just a hired killer. We want the man that paid him. We have been working on this for five years, we think we know who ordered the killing but we need more evidence."

"We came to Chicago thinking you could be the killer."

"That's what we were afraid of. You asking questions about me could get me killed if the wrong people find out I was with your father and that there was a connection between your father and myself."

"Who do you think is behind this?" Denise was on the edge of her chair waiting for his reply.

Foster looked at Paul Wheeler before he responded. "Well, nothing happens in this town without the blessing of Mike McDonald but he could have just stepped aside and let somebody else do it."

"What would you have us do?" James was more relaxed, he spoke as he took a chair beside Denise.

"We could maybe use your help. We have a large old home, The Winton House. It is the center of our operation in Chicago. We print up reports to send to Washington. We have several empty rooms, we could pay you a little and give you board and room. James could work as a driver, help out in the stable. You could write reports, set type and print reports. We could maybe even use you from time to time to do some undercover work."

"That would be great as we are running low on funds." James turned to Denise to see if she agreed.

"Yes. I want to do anything to help find out who ordered this. I am a little relieved to learn that the man that killed my father is dead."

"Paul will take you to the Winton House and get you settled. If you should meet me on the street you don't know me any more than any of the other fans. We need to get you some new duds, you tend to stand out and that draws attention."

Back at the hotel they had gathered their things and were walking out. "Were you surprised at that?"

"Surprised? I felt like my aunt Helen when she was genuinely surprised, she would say, 'Butter my buns and call me a biscuit'."

James almost dropped his bags, he was glad he was following her so that she didn't see his reaction to her comment. She never ceased to amaze him.

CHAPTER NINE

In the basement of the Winton House they had a firing range it was a short indoor range of fifty feet. It was set up so they could fire both rifles and hand guns. They had a table full of weapons: The Burnside Carbine, The Henry repeater, Smith and Wesson 38DA revolver, nickel plated that just came out that year, a Colt 1860 Army Model with a long eight inch barrel, the Peacemaker Colt .45 caliber, and a Smith & Wesson top break revolver that the barrel tipped down and ejected all empty shells at once.

"I want to get an idea of how you handle a weapon." Paul Wheeler had asked Denise and James to follow him to the basement. "James, you first. All these weapons are loaded, pick out one of the hand guns and fire a round at that target."

James pick up the Peacemaker Colt .45 Caliber single action. He thumbed back the hammer, held the gun at arm's length and fired a round into the center of the bull's eye.

"Good. Now hold the weapon at your side, and shoot a round from your hip."

James did as was instructed and again found the center of the bull's eye.

"Excellent, it is easy to see that you have grown up around fire arms. Denise you want to pick out a weapon and do the same as James."

She choose the Smith & Wesson 38DA revolver. Her first shot at arm's length was dead center. From the hip she was a little off center but still in the bull's eye.

"Excellent, again it is easy to see that you are comfortable firing the revolver. We need to know these things in case it is ever necessary for you to protect yourselves. You will be able to come down here and practice. Do you have weapons of your own?"

"I have Denise's fathers Modele 1873 double action revolver." James produced the weapon from his coat pocket.

"I have a Remington, .41 caliber derringer." Denise took it from her duster pocket and held it in the palm of her hand. "Not real good at this distance but I can still put the slug near the bull's eye."

"Those are both fine. Like I said, you can come down here and practice with any of these and if you are going out in the field you can use any that you think you will need."

The Winton House was located on an acre of land with a high stone fence all around and a wrought iron gate leading out to Lake Shore Drive. It had been owned and built by Charles Winton who moved back to England after losing his only son in the Civil War. He sold it to Chicago Brick and Tile, which was a shell company for the Treasury Department. It was a three story brick building, six bedrooms and three bathrooms. A large kitchen, dining room on the first floor with office space and a bathroom. The second floor was the print shop, an office, two bed rooms and a bathroom. The third floor was four bedrooms and a bath. They had a full time chef and housekeeper.

Denise had a room on the second floor, the men had rooms on the third floor. Not all of those that worked at the Winton House lived there. Some had families and went home each night.

The stable had room for six horses, at the present time they had four and two surreys. Both carriages had two seats, a top and curtains. A Negro, Mose was the head driver and in charge of the stable. James found him very easy to work for and very good at what he did.

Denise worked in the print shop with two men. John Anderson was tall and skinny, you could almost hear his bones rattle when he moved. His hollow eyes and pale skin made him seem older than his thirty-six years. Dustin Wolfgram was in charge. He was of average height and weight and if he didn't wear a visor his blond hair was always in his eyes. He was not happy, he wanted to be in the field, running the print shop was not what he signed up for.

Denise soon learned they were doing more than just working on solving her father's murder. There were a large number of Chicago and Gary Indiana companies that held government contracts. Some of them were over charging for their products or shipping inferior products. She had to read all the agent notes and put them in type for the reports to Washington. She learned about everything that was going on in the investigations. It was not long and they felt like a part of the organization and family of Winton House. They did not get to be part of the arrests or taking the people to jail, this was done by the police or federal agents working with the police. In this way they could continue to work with known criminals they did not have enough evidence to make an arrest.

Days passed and summer turned into fall. The baseball season was over and now the wind coming off Lake Michigan could be super cold. They both had to purchase new winter clothing as they had none. Mr. Wheeler gave them both suggestions of what to buy and what not to buy.

As Mr. Wheeler gained confidence in their ability to handle situations they became very busy. As Mose would say, "Busier than a cat trying to bury its poop on a marble floor."

CHAPTER TEN

Now that the season was over, Red Foster had a great amount of free time. He still had a few things to do each day to prepare for the upcoming season. A few players to get signed, new uniforms to order and events to attend but for the most part his days were free. The team had enjoyed a great season, winning the National League Pennant with a team record of 67 wins and just 17 loses.

As the player/manager, Red was the toast of the town. His money was no good anywhere in the city. He ordered a drink and somebody wanted to pay for it. The same if he went to a nice restaurant to eat. He had more invites to parties and dinners than he could ever hope to attend. There was always a business man wanting to set him up with a sister or cousin.

Thomas Palmer had purchased land that was mostly swamp after the Great Chicago Fire of 1871. He had started a dry-goods business with Marshall Field and Levi Leiter. Chicago was the fastest growing city of the time, it grew from three hundred thousand in 1870 to nearly a million by 1880.

The Gold Coast and the Lincoln Park neighborhood, were the treasured residential areas in Chicago. This was where the high society lived. It mattered little how you made your money, just that you had money. Mike McDonald, Mayor Carter Harrison Sr., Thomas Palmer, and Red Foster were all welcomed to the same parties.

In 1876 reform candidate Harvey Calvin had been elected Mayor but using his power and money, Mike McDonald got his man Carter Harrison Sr. elected in 1879.

It was at these cocktail parties that many of the decisions that affected Chicago's future were made. Mass production, the railroad making travel and shipping faster as well as more convenient, lead to economic prosperity. McDonald had control of Chicago and Gary

Indiana's bookmaking rights. He had learned the value of paying protection and having his men in positions of power in the city. He also had learned how to keep his hands clean. He insulated himself from anything shady so he was thought of in the same way as Palmer, Field, and Leiter.

"Will the White Stockings have as good a season has they enjoyed last year?"

"Well, as you know, we have led the league in doubles because of our short right field fence. The team management will change the ground rules to make the entire outfield fence a homerun. This past season we hit fifteen homeruns, you can look for that number to triple for this coming season." Red took a sip from his drink.

"The city is thinking strongly of reclaiming the land of Lake Front Park and building a new park on the west side." Mayor Harrison was a fan and held a box seat at the Lake Front Park.

"We had heard that, and being the homerun is the most popular aspect of our game, we want to make this last season spectacular."

"Will this make a difference in your team's success?" McDonald asked what seemed to be an innocent question.

"We will load our team with players that can hit the long ball to right field. We play half our games in Lake Front Park, all the other teams play twelve games there. It will make us lead the league in homeruns."

This conversation was important to many in different ways. To McDonald for gambling reasons, to Palmer if he could figure out where the new park would be built, and to Field and Leiter if this changed the traffic to their store. Just because they were at a party did not mean they were not working, not planning for their future.

Red Foster was working too, he would let Mr. Wheeler know of this conversation and see if it led to any changes in activity. With the new ball park there would be new contracts. Which brewery would get the beer contract, which vender would get the food and which construction company would get to build the new park. There was so much money to be made.

Red Foster had learned that as long as he didn't ask any questions he could listen in on most any conversation without drawing any attention to himself. From time to time he would ask Denise to accompany him so that they could learn what the women were talking about. Red had a couple other lady friends that he would escort from time to time to keep the gossip to a minimum. This also tended to keep the wolves from nipping at his heels.

They were on their way back to the Brown Hotel, James was driving their surrey. They would drop Denise at the hotel and then James would drive Red home and later Mose would come and pick up Denise.

"Did you learn anything tonight?"

"Mrs. Palmer made an attempt to find out from Mrs. Harrison if she knew where the new baseball park would be. I did notice Mrs. McDonald seemed to be very interested in what Mrs. Harrison had to say."

"I didn't learn much but I did pass on a little confidential information about the team that could cause some new developments. I appreciate you going with me, hope you don't mind."

"No, I enjoy seeing how the other half live and hoping that I can learn a little to help solve my father's murder."

"We never know what could be a connection and what that connection might be to the big picture. That is why it is important to write down everything we can think of the conversations. When they look at your notes and compare them to my notes, something could pop up that would give us a new lead."

"Yes, it does amaze me when you add in what James learns from talking with the other drivers what can jump out at you."

"Do you and James have a special relationship?"

"James walked into my life. He said I am here for you and proved it with his actions. Yes, we have a special relationship but have not been romantic."

CHAPTER ELEVEN

The Western Union messenger knocked on the door of the Winton House. This was not unusual as they would often get a wire. Today was different as the message was for James.

"Thanks stop good to hear from you stop we are fine stop" It was signed, Jokob.

Earlier James had sent them a wire over the Denver Pacific Railroad and Telegraph Company to his father at the Denver rail station. He had hoped that his father would stop in just to check and see if there were any messages. Apparently he had and sent one back to his son.

James had sent them his address and now that he knew they had received it he could expect a letter in the mail. With the railroads now carrying the mail, the Pony Express was discontinued.*

James would have to take the time to write his folks a letter and explain more in detail what he was doing. He had come to really enjoy working at the Winton House and had received several hours of training from Mr. Wheeler and Mose. It was a case of things not to do more than what to do as they always had to react to situations. As they gained confidence in his ability he was given more missions.

* The Pony express only lasted eighteen months but it made for some interesting dime novels.

It was when he was on one of these missions that he found Edna. He had been sent to The Store on Hair-trigger Block. He was to go to the Casino on the second floor and gamble with some counterfeit bills. Hoping that they would spot the bills and then want to know where he got them. The problem was, the bills appeared too genuine and no one spotted them before he ran out and was forced to leave.

He went to his rig and that is when he saw Edna hiding on the floor of the surrey. Her sad, no-one-loves-me eyes held his attention so that he did not notice her clothing. He did not want to make a scene here and call attention to himself so he pretended not to see her. He had been told not to drive back to the Winton House in case he was followed. His instructions were to drive to a stable on Wabash and then walk back to the Winton House making at least one stop on his way.

His mind was racing with what he should do. It was plain to see that this young girl was hiding and being that his rig had been parked at The Store his first thought was that she was hiding from someone that was at or worked at The Store. He did not want anyone that may be at the stable to see her, so he did what he thought was the best thing to do.

"I am going to continue to drive for a while in case anyone is following us." He knew she could hear him but there was no reply.

"I don't know who you are hiding from but you can trust me to help you if I can." Again there was only silence from the floor of the surrey.

"My name is James, what is yours?" Still not a peep out of the girl.

"Would you like for me to drive you some place?" He turned onto Lake Shore Drive as there were several parks and places where young lovers went to look at the lake and spoon.

"I have a lady friend that will help you. Do you want me to drive you to her place?" He had drove in a circle and had not seen anyone following them. He could get himself in trouble with Mr. Wheeler if he took her to the Winton House and she was not who he thought she was.

"What would you like for me to do?" They were at a spot on the lake where there were no homes for more than a block in any direction. He could not see any other rigs, so he pulled the horse up. He didn't know why she mysteriously showed up in his surrey and she wasn't talking.

"If you don't talk to me, I can't help you. Do you want me to drive you to the police station?"

"No!" He could hear her moving but could not see her from his position on the driving seat.

"Do you have family in Chicago?"

"No."

"Where are you from?"

"Nowhere."

"What do you mean?"

"I used to be from somewhere, but I'm not from anywhere now."

"What where you doing at The Store?"

"I had been working on the floor at the casino selling drinks but they said I needed to earn more money to pay for my costume so they put me in a room on the fourth floor." Her voice trailed off so that James could scarcely hear her final words.

"What is your name?"

"Edna but at The Store they called me Kitten."

"I have some friends that would like to hear your story and will help you."

"Are they police?"

"No. Why do you ask?"

"Because the police work with the men at The Store."

"They won't turn you over to the police or take you back to The Store." James waited for her to decide if she could trust him.

"Who are these friends of yours?"

James didn't know how much he could tell her and how much he should tell her. If he told her they were federal agents that could scare her off. He felt it would be safe to drive back to the Winton House and he felt sure that Mr. Wheeler would like to hear her story. But what if she was not who she said she was. What if they had her hide in his rig to learn who he was? He felt certain that the fear and sadness he saw in her eyes was real. Now James had to decide if he could trust her.

He remembered his father saying, "The devil always dresses up evil and makes it look good." Could this be one of those times?

CHAPTER TWELVE

Edna proved to be interesting but not of a great deal of help to them or their case. She did not know McDonald, had never seen a man by that name or heard his name spoken. It was a man they called Kelly and Big Sal a woman that she remembered. She came to Chicago from a small town in Wisconsin, Appleton. Mr. Wheeler helped her to get back to the town she wanted to get away from just weeks before.

James was about to go back with some more counterfeit bills to see if he could get them interested.

"Walk up to the Brown, and take a cab to The Store. The dealers may have given the description of the man passing the phony money to the pit boss so look for them to approach you. We will have a man in there before you get there to back you up if needed." Mr. Wheeler handed James a roll of the fake bills.

James took the bills and put them in his pants pocket. He was dressed in the latest fashion. A well-tailored frock coat with matching trousers cut with a straight leg and no pressed crease. His Bo Hat matched his coat and pants.

"Foster will also be in the casino but do not act like you know him. He will just be there to observe. If they take the bait and want you to produce more bills for them, don't seem too eager. Good luck."

James walked in the back door of the Brown Hotel, through the lobby and out the front door. He walked up to the first cab in line. It was boxy with two wheels, pulled by one horse. It had an elevated driver's seat behind the cab.

"I would like to go to the nearest casino." The driver a small man getting up in years, opened the cab door for James to enter.

"That would be The Store, just a few blocks north of here." He closed the door and mounted the back of his cab. He made a clucking sound. His horse moved away from the curb and headed up the street.

James paid the driver with some good coins. The fake money was only for the casino. In the casino he found his way to a blackjack table and gave the dealer a fake twenty for some chips. He had just been dealt his cards when he felt a tap on his shoulder.

"Would you please come with me sir?" James turned to see a large man with scars over both his eye brows and cauliflower ears. He appeared to have been a bare knuckle boxer that had not been good at the trade. He stepped back and made a sweeping motion with his right hand.

"Let me finish this hand." James turned back to his cards. This time the hand gripped his shoulder, fingers digging into the muscle.

"The dealer will take care of your cards. Come with me."

He was almost lifted off the stool. He would have fell backward had it not been for the man's grip holding him up. They walked around the roulette table toward a door marked, "Office." A man standing to the side of the door opened it for them to pass.

Inside were several men. The man seated behind the huge oak desk was going over some sheets of paper laid out before him. He was a good looking, well-dressed man with hair colored like rust. He had a large diamond ring on the little finger of his left hand. He lifted his eyes from the papers and studied James for a few seconds before speaking.

"You're new in town?"

"Yeah, just been here a few days." James could not help but notice the large safe in the corner of the room, and the fact that the room did not have a window.

"Where you come from." The man had a slight accent but nothing so strong that James could pin point what it was.

"St. Louis." Again, the man studied James before he spoke.

"What's your name?"

"Jon, Jon Hamsun."

"Let me tell you a few things Jon Hamsun. We run an honest gambling casino, we don't water the whiskey, and we don't prostitute the women. We don't cheat our customers and we don't allow them to cheat us." He now took a twenty dollar bill from one of the men and dropped in on the desk in front of him.

"You bring this with you from St. Louis?" His steel blue eyes were on those of James.

"Yes." James nodded toward the bill as he spoke.

"You got any honest money on you?"

Again, James nodded as he said, "Yes".

"You got any friends here with you?"

"No, I'm alone."

"This is what is going to happen. My man is going to take you to Union Station where you will buy a ticket to St. Louis. He will wait for you to board the train. Don't come back to Chicago." His eyes continued to look deep into those of James, as if he were reading his soul.

"What about my things at the hotel?" They had set the room up at the Brown, with some dirty clothes and some more counterfeit money. They also had a small hole in the wall behind one of the pictures where they could see into the room.

"Count yourself lucky to get out of town with your cheating hide." He nodded to one of the men who stepped forward to take James by the arm.

"You can tell any friends you have in St. Louis that Chicago is not the place to come with fake money." When they had gone out the door, McDonald turned to another man. "Go to the Brown, find out his room number and bring back any and all the stuff belonging to this Jon Hamsun. I want to see every scrap of paper, every dirty sock."

CHAPTER THIRTEEN

Kankakee was the first stop out of Chicago. James got up and got off the train. Looking around the station he saw a barber shop with a barber sitting in the chair reading a newspaper.

"Can I get a haircut?" James asked as he walked in the shop. His hair was long, covering his ears.

"Have a seat, got it all warmed up for you." The barber looked to be Italian and his accent confirmed it.

"Need you to lower my ears and remove the stache." James climbed into the chair and the barber swung a cloth over him and fastened it tight behind his neck.

"You sure you want me to take your mustache? Looks awful nice and full."

"Yeah, going home to see my folks and my mom doesn't like long hair or a mustache." He wanted to change his appearance as much as possible in case the man was still at the Union Station waiting to see if he came back.

When the barber took the cloth off him fifteen minutes later and James handed him a quarter and a nickel tip he intentionally forgot his derby on the shelf. He hoped the new haircut, no mustache and a bare head would be enough to make him no longer Jon Hamsun.

The train ride back to Chicago was uneventful. Walking north from Union Station, James was as cold as he could ever remember. This wind off Lake Michigan seemed to bite to the bone. True he was not dressed as he had been in Colorado, and his bare head and new haircut didn't help, but he was about froze when he got to the Winton House.

"What happened to your mustache? I liked your mustache." Denise looked up from her work as James entered. Mr. Wheeler also turned to see a very cold James.

James told them of what had happened to him in the last eight hours. "Either McDonald is a very good liar or he doesn't know everything his employees are doing. Myself, I don't think he would lie."

"Why do you say that?" Denise handed him a fresh cup of coffee to help warm him up.

"Edna told us about this Kelly and Big Sal and McDonald said, we run an honest gambling casino, we don't water the whiskey, and we don't prostitute the women."

"Do you think Edna was telling us a story?"

"No. I think there is no honor among thieves. I only saw McDonald for a few minutes but he does not appear to be the type that would send a man to St. Louis to kill your father."

"That is how Red Foster perceives him too." Mr. Wheeler took a cup of coffee from Denise. "I didn't say anything because I didn't want to influence your thinking."

"To think I had this all figured out when I got on the train in St. Louis." Denise slumped back into her chair.

"That is how investigations go. You have to keep an open mind and not overlook any valuable piece to the puzzle. Write up everything that you saw and heard. Red will be sending what he saw if anything and so will agent Smithson. Sometimes it becomes a process of elimination."

"Oh, James a letter came for you. It is over there with the other mail. It is from your mother." Denise pointed toward the library table.

James was anxious to hear the news from Eagle Valley but at the same time he could not see himself going back there to live. He liked what he was doing. He had to admit that he liked the city. He liked his new friends and he liked the adrenaline rush he got when on a mission.

He guessed that he missed his family but had to admit that days, even weeks would pass without him thinking of them. Did that mean he was not a good man? Did that mean he was selfish, that all he cared about was himself? Was it normal for a person to get so involved in what was going on around them that they didn't think of family miles away? When he was in the valley all he could think about was Denise.

He took the letter and settled into a chair to read the news. It was not a long letter, just one page. His mother had never talked just to be talking and he guessed that she would write the news in as few words as possible.

He noticed the stamp. A three cent Washington stamp and the post mark was from Bear Lake. They had not had a post office in Bear Lake the last time he was there. He would write them a letter but he would not tell them everything that was going on. His mother would just worry if she knew what he was doing. He wondered if not telling everything was the same as telling a lie.

November 15, 1880

My Dearest James,

Thanksgiving is almost here and we have so much to be thankful for. Your brother Kemp and Pat have a baby girl. Caroline Kaye is beautiful. Kemp is such a proud father and Luta is a very good big brother.

Chet and Dusty are growing like weeds and tend to be Tintypes of their fathers. Sarah is a miniature Judith which upsets Judith from time to time. Martha, I am the only one who calls her that, to everyone else she is Squirt. She is learning from Sarah and Chet how to get what she wants from her parents.

We can get mail now at Bear Lake. Just send it to us in care of general delivery and they will hold it until we come in.

You know the pair of eagles that were always on that dead tree up on the bluff? I have not seen them since you rode out of the valley.

All My Love
Mother

"How are things with your folks?"

"Good and I am an uncle."

"Uncle James, that make you want to get on the train and head back to Colorado?"

"No. I'm happy with where I am. Once she gets old enough to know who I am, I want to see her. Babies are all about the same to me. Does that make me a bad person?"

"No, I remember my father saying, never reply when you're angry, never make a promise when you're happy and never make a decision when you're sad. And then he would look at me and say, and above all, never say never."

Chapter Fourteen

Charles Wilcox was a lanky good-looking man who had fought for the Confederacy during the Civil War. He and his intelligent, strikingly beautiful wife came north as the south was in such a mess. The only thing of value they had besides the clothes on their backs was a bourbon mash whiskey recipe. These directions for preparing this sweeter, fuller alcohol proved to be all they needed to succeed in Chicago.

The rye whiskey made by all the distillers in Chicago from at least 51 percent rye was not near as popular as the bourbon distilled from at least 51 percent corn.

Layla Mae Wilcox had used her charm to get them a stake. They started in a small building where they also lived. Selling it a bottle at a time to the bars and speakeasies. But it was not long and many of the customers were asking for their Dixie bourbon by name. They expanded, getting workers to do the labor while they did the selling and the promoting.

Being able to siphon off the federal liquor taxes put them over the ledge and made them part of Chicago's high society. Their mansion in the Lincoln Park neighborhood and a modern distillery on the south side made them part of the establishment.

McDonald's Democrat party and his mayor Carter Harrison Sr. were in power. But there was another political party in Chicago that was growing in power. They were anti-immigration, anti-liquor.

They wanted to ban liquor sales on Sunday, which would hurt the White Stockings as the fans did not want to attend the games on Sunday if they could not enjoy a beer.

At this time Chicago was made mostly of Germans, Irish and Scandinavians. A few English, Italians and Poles. Chicago had some of the most progressive anti-discrimination laws in the nation.

Because of this and the need for unskilled labor in the packing houses, the black population was growing fast. Mayor Harrison was the head of the Common Council of Alderman. Politics tends to make for strange bed fellows sometimes. Seated at the large dinner table were the Harrison's, the McDonald's, the Wilcox's, the Palmer's, Red Foster and Denise. The table talk was not of politics, but of the theater and baseball. Later they would break up into two groups, the men would have a drink and a cigar to enjoy while they talked shop.

Later in their surrey, Red and Denise compared notes on the evening. "McDonald would rather solve problems with a bribe than with force. But I didn't get that same feeling about Wilcox."

"I got the same feeling about his wife. She looks so pretty and sweet but the comments she made about the farmers market were not sugar and honey. She made it very clear that the smell of the rotting vegetables and horse droppings was not acceptable."

"Funny you should say that. Her husband also made a comment on the farmers market."

"Think they could have an interest in expanding their business?"

"I don't know. When you write up your report be sure to include that. The Market is made up of hundreds of individual venders, it would be as difficult to organize them as it is to get them to pick up their trash."

They were pulling up in front of the Winton House, their driver, Mose opened the door for Denise and helped her step down. Most of the house was dark, there was a light in the front entrée and another up on the third floor.

"James, are you awake?" Denise could see the light coming from under his door.

"Yes, come in. I was just writing a letter to my parents. It is so difficult to write when there is so much you don't want them to know." He was sitting up in bed with his half written letter. "How did it go?"

"It was a nice dinner but I don't think we learned that much. Red thinks McDonald is the type that would rather bribe than use force."

"But the question would be, what would he do if a bribe did not work? We both would never believe that he could bribe your father."

"That's true and he is used to getting his way." She moved to the edge of his bed and reaching over and touched his upper lip. "You look so different without your mustache."

He didn't plan it, he didn't even know he was going to do it. It just was a reflex action. He kissed her finger. She was surprised but as always not caught off balance.

"It's a start." She said, with a smile. She turned and went to her room, leaving James with a "What was that" look on his face.

CHAPTER FIFTEEN

James saw what in his mind's eye was a bears head and the bear was about to harm a small calf. He took aim, squeezed the trigger and the Modele 1873 jumped in his hand. A small dot appeared between the eyes and the bear's arms flew into the air. The force of the slug slamming it back and out of sight. His double action revolver swung to another target.

But it wasn't a bear in the valley in Colorado, it was a man in a warehouse in Chicago.

Hands were going up in the air, the gun fight was over.

"Nothing ends a gun fight like a slug between the eyes of one of the leaders. That was a nice shot James." Wheeler and Smithson moved quickly to arrest the men.

James thought he would be sick, it was the first time he had ever killed a man. As a boy, on the wagon train, he had shot in the direction of some men but had never hit one. He had seen Wade and others shoot and kill but this was different. This was him, he was the one that pulled the trigger. He was the one that took a life.

They had raided an unlawful oleomargarine plant, on the south side. Some of these moonshine plants would actually make the spread out of beef fats and cow's milk. This one purchased good quality oleo from Armour, added a yellow food color to the white oleo and sold it for butter making a huge profit.

They had heard cries for help from both Armour and the dairy industry to say nothing of the customers that were getting deceived. Like moonshine whiskey, moonshine butter was made in unsanitary conditions. It would often cause sickness or death because of contamination.

They had hoped to catch one of the leaders but like so often when they raided a still, it was only the workers that were arrested. They would question them, even offer them a chance to walk if they would implicate their boss. They knew the chances of this happening were slim and none.

The dead man appeared to be Irish. All but one of the others were black. It was a good bet they could neither read nor write. After the Civil war, missionary groups and churches worked to give this emancipated population the opportunity to learn. Former slaves of every age took advantage of this to become literate. Grandfathers and their grandchildren sat together in the classrooms seeking to obtain the tools to make a better life. But there were so many to teach and so few to teach them.

Some of the oleo was still in the Amour boxes. Some had already been colored, wrapped in a wax paper and put in butter boxes labeled Lake Michigan Cheese and Butter. This warehouse was in a largely black neighborhood which had little if any police patrol. Many of the owners would hire a watchman or turn a dog or two loose in their warehouses at night.

The Department of Treasury's function was to assess and collect fees and penalties and to intercept and seize counter band. They did not have a jail or detention center to hold prisoners. They would often work with the Chicago Police but tonight they were working alone because the last couple of times the criminals had been tipped off and they found nothing.

They separated the men and questioned them one at a time. Many of the blacks coming north after they were freed faced daunting challenges. They were mostly illiterate knowing little of the world beyond the plantation of their birth. These men tended to fall into that mold but it was often difficult to tell as they would frequently play dumb.

None of the blacks had a weapon, only the dead man and the other white man. After an hour of questions they had learned very little. They had the men load all the oleo and fake butter on the wagons that were in the warehouse. The dead man was placed in their wagon and would be taken to the morgue. The oleo would be burned. They kept a few packages of the white oleo and a few of the fake butter to take back to the Winton House with them.

A search of the place turned up nothing that would help in their investigation. Smithson went to the nearest police call box to have a paddy wagon sent to the warehouse.

James had been walking around in a daze but he was starting to get some color back in his face and the nauseous feeling was going away. Mr. Wheeler came up to him and put a hand on his shoulder.

"Your action most likely saved at least one other life and maybe one of our lives. If you need to talk just knock on my door. This is a part of our job that none of us like but it is a part that happens."

James did not sleep well. He could not turn his mind off and relax. He kept seeing it over and over. One time it would be the Irishmen and the next time it would be the bear. He knew that Wheeler was right, that it had been necessary and that it could have saved a life. But that did not help him relax and fall to sleep.

Denise was looking at some papers and sipping on a cup of coffee when James walked in the next morning. He looked like he had not slept all night.

"How you doing?" She asked looking up from her papers.

"I'm okay."

"You do know James that you can't pick up a dog turd by the clean end. Looks like this job is sometimes that same way." James didn't know if he were more surprised at what she said or the nonchalant way she said it. But he did understand the meaning, sometimes this job was dirty, difficult and dangerous.

CHAPTER SIXTEEN

Most of the men at the millionaires table at the Chicago Club lunch thought all women were physically weak, vulnerable and intellectually inferior to men. That is why they couldn't vote, hold political office or even attend a major league baseball game unless escorted by a man.

Now the Chicago White Stocking baseball club was going to have a ladies day where both escorted and unescorted women would be allowed into the park free. This was the team's fourth season playing at Lakefront Park and if things worked as planned, it would be their last.

The team was making plans for their spring barnstorming tour to get the team ready for the 1881 season. The pitchers and catchers had been throwing in a warehouse for a couple weeks. Infielders had been taking ground balls.

Red Foster would take fifteen men on the train. Four pitchers, two catchers, five infielders and four outfielders. They would play college and semi-pro teams in Georgia and Mississippi on their way to New Orleans.

Traveling by train at night and playing games during the day. Their share of the gate would pay their expenses, or at least they hoped it would. To most of the people in these towns, the sight of a major league player was a novelty. One they would pay good hard cash to see. There was no organized spring training for the National League, this was their way to get the team ready for the season. They were the National League defending champions and the team and the city hoped they could repeat this feat in 1881.

In another part of the city the Chicago Women's Club was meeting. They would have luncheon programs, afternoon teas and on occasions evening dinners. They would have book discussions, play bridge, and even have a guest speaker from time to time speak on investments.

Layla Mae Wilcox was gaining in power and stature within the club. She had just been voted in as vice-president. Her professional and social position was making her an important woman in Chicago. She was far from weak and intellectually inferior to men. Mrs. Goldsmith was the president but it was Layla who made the important decisions involving the club.

"The White Stockings are going to have a Ladies Day at the ball park this season. We should make plans to go as a club. We could get box seats and make an afternoon of it. I understand they will be admitting women into the park free, but I think we should up grade and get the box seats." Layla waited, thinking that someone would object. When no one did, she added. "I think it is important for us to promote women's rights. This is just a small step, but it is a change in the right direction."

After a short discussion they voted and it carried without opposition. They would have a sign-up sheet in order to know how many seats they would require. They would meet for lunch first and then go to the game as a group. Mrs. Goldsmith would check to see if they could get a special group rate on the box seats.

The Wilcox's were just starting to sell their six year old bourbon. By law it had to be labeled with the age of the youngest whiskey in the bottle. But this did not keep them from cheating a little. They developed a green bottle with a porcelain stopper which was latched with a wire over the lip of the bottle. This green bottle seemed to give their bourbon an expensive look. They could make a great deal more selling it by the bottle rather than by the barrel.

It was not long and they were shipping their Dixie Bourbon all over the nation and it was becoming a top shelf bourbon. The demand was so great for their six year old bourbon that some of the three year old doubled in age overnight.

Layla Mae and her husband Charles were millionaires and with this came power. They had hit Chicago at the right time. Got their business going in time to jump ahead being able to siphon off thousands in federal liquor taxes. They had learned a few tricks from one of the best to ever make whiskey. Yeast grown on sorghum made better whiskey than yeast grown on corn. Corn was a sweet grain and the greater percentage used, the sweeter the whiskey. Prior to aging if it was filtered through charcoal chips made from sugar maple timbers, it was smoother sipping.

They were forced from time to time to make a poor grade to pay the bills and buy supplies. They managed to do this and not have it traced to their label. This was marketed under Chicago's Best. Only the better tasting whiskey was Dixie Bourbon.

Layla Mae was the brains and Charles the muscle as they made money hand over fist. They did however, lose several hundred when the federal agents hit the warehouse. It was their operation. They lost the cost of the oleo they purchased, the cost of making it look like butter and the profit they would have made on the deal.

The loss of the man was minor, he could be replaced. They could not even complain to McDonald as he did not know it was their operation. They had failed to get his blessing when expanding. They would just have to bite the bullet, accept the situation and move on.

They had been moving on in the right direction. Now they were reaping the harvest of their efforts and even expanding into other areas of opportunity. They were doing all this and at the same time making friends with the better people of Chicago.

CHAPTER SEVENTEEN

The Chicago White Stocking baseball team had to switch trains and this gave them a short lay over in St. Louis. It was long enough for Red to meet with Collins. They exchanged information and Red gave him the address at the Winton House where he could write Denise.

"The one good thing that came from those two being in St. Louis was that I got to know Sgt. Miner. He has been very helpful, he is a good man." Collins was taking notes as if he were interviewing the manager of the Chicago White Stockings, not talking to a fellow Federal Agent. He would write a short article about the team in tomorrow's paper, the stakes were too high in this game to take any chances.

"Yes, and the good thing that came from them coming to Chicago is that they are both good people. They have fit in well." Red and the team were headed to cities in Georgia, Tennessee, Mississippi and ending up in New Orleans. He would be rubbing elbows with some of the most powerful men in the south on both sides of the law.

I bit of information here, added to a name or date could prove to be of importance. Red was a good listener and people loved to talk and impress him. It would take him a half hour or longer each night before bed to make notes of what he had learned. He would send his notes once a week to the Winton House. They were working on many different federal cases and many times these cases were linked together.

It was in Jackson, Tennessee, a small city half way between Nashville and Memphis that he was asked the question. They were talking about whiskey, bourbon and some of the people that produced the best. "Have you run across Lila Mae Lewis in Chicago?

"No, I can't say that I know anyone by that name."

"If you had you would remember. She is strikingly beautiful, and just as ruthless as she is pretty. She came from a family down here that made some great tasting whiskey. They were ruined in the war and the last I heard she had gone north to Chicago."

"Why do you say she is as ruthless as she is pretty?"

"The whiskey business in Tennessee is like no other business. It is very competitive, one rival will do anything and everything to make the best whiskey. During the war, the south prohibited bourbon distilling. Partly because the corn was needed to feed the soldiers and because they wanted the copper from the stills so they could turn the copper into cannons. Her father was killed in the war and she took over the Old Arsenal Brewery."

"You seem to know this family well."

"Jackson is small, I was young, too young to get involved but not too young to listen and learn what was going on."

"So, why did this Lila Mae leave?"

"Confederate soldiers came to the Old Arsenal for the copper and as the story goes, she killed one of them."

"So you think she ran north?"

"The north continued to make whiskey and they taxed it. I have heard that the whiskey tax supported their war effort. Whiskey making was in her blood, if she couldn't make it down here, she would go where she could make it."

"She sounds like an interesting woman. Like you say, one I would remember if I had met her. Anything else about her that stood out?"

"I don't remember ever seeing her, as I said I was young. But at the time she was the talk of the town." He took a sip of his drink. He had played outfield on the semi-pro team the White Stockings had beat earlier in the afternoon. They were now at a cookout for the teams at the home of the mayor.

There had been a good crowd at the game and they still had a couple hours before they had to catch their train to Memphis where they would play tomorrow.

Red was thinking later on the train about what the young man had told him. Writing his notes he remembered something he had heard. "It's easier to fool people than to convince them they have been fooled."*

*This quote is credited to Mark Twain.

CHAPTER EIGHTEEN

Mr. Sun was just coming up with ribbons of silver and gold on Lake Michigan as James hitched Old Ned to the surrey. Old Ned was getting long in the tooth and had traveled more miles on the streets of Chicago than any horse in the stable and maybe any horse in the city. A big black gelding with three white socks, he carried his head high and proud.

James filled a feed bag with oats and put it under the driver's seat. He had no idea how long they would be, could be an hour and it could be for all day. They were going to Haymarket, a farmers market where produce from all around Chicago was bought to be sold or traded. If it had any value at all, you could find it at Haymarket.

Denise would walk and shop while James would listen to other driver's gossip. This idle talk would often produce something of value. Many of the driver's liked to talk about their people and their affairs. It would often get to the point of, can you top this. Of course it was not always true but often the truth was stranger than the fiction. Once in a while even the fiction had an element of truth to it.

It was mid-morning when James spotted the Wilcox driver matching pennies with another driver. It was not long and the Wilcox driver had won all the pennies and he turned to look for another victim.

"Got any pennies you would like to wager?" He asked looking at James.

"May have a few. You like match or unlike?" James reached in his pocket for some coins.

"I'm like you, I win." He said ready to flip his penny.

"Okay." James agreed his copper ready to flip.

The first time they were both heads and James lost. But the next two times James won. They went back and forth, neither winning more than a couple times in a row.

"You drive the missies here today?" James asked in between flips.

"You kidding? She came once, said between the stinking of rotting vegetables and horse droppings she would never come again. She sends the house keeper with a list of things to buy."

"They pretty nice people to drive for?"

"Mr. Charles is fine, she can be very demanding."

"I like to hear her talk. Such a pretty woman with that southern accent." James had just lost three times in a row and was down to his last copper.

"What's on the inside is different than what you see on the outside. She is the boss, she runs the company. She tells him what to do and what not to do. He gives all the orders but they come from her. She knows her whiskey, she is very shrewd."

"How long have you been driving for them?"

"Just since the first of the year. I was working in the distillery, they put a sign up on the bulletin board for a driver and I got the job. This is much better than mixing the mash."

"What happened to the driver they had?"

"Don't know. No one seems to know. One day he just didn't show up."

"Do you know what his name was?"

"I heard, can't recall…. seems like it was Irish. Patrick something."

"You cleaned me out. You always this lucky?" James held out his hands palms up.

"I have been on a roll. Good breaks have been coming my way. I have been picking up a little extra money working over time."

"Good for you. It is always nice to earn a little extra."

"Yeah, my Pa always said to look out for the pennies and the pounds would look after themselves."

CHAPTER NINETEEN

They were just a half hour northwest of the Winton House and it looked like a different world. The narrow dirt road followed the Fox River as it wound its way through the country side. The last house they passed was at least a mile behind them. Coming around a bend they saw the majestic flight of a bald eagle. It must have had a wingspan of six feet.

Such a noble bird, it carried a fish in a talon and seeing the white head and tail they knew it was an adult bird. They had a great view of the bird in flight as it followed the river. Both of their minds drifted back to days in Colorado.

James could see the nest in a tall Spruce on the high south bluff as he came out the door of their cabin. Next to it was a dead Ponderosa Pine that the birds liked to sit in. James would often stand and watch the eagles. The eagle is sensitive to man and man's activity while nesting but at this distance they showed no sign of fear. He watched as the eagle took off from the dead tree branch. In just seconds it was soaring on the thermal currents high above the valley.

As Sister Denise walked in the court yard of the mission she looked up to see an eagle soaring high overhead. She wondered what it would feel like to be so free, so powerful. The eagle was such a stately, dignified, symbol of freedom. She had been so discombobulated the last few months. Like the eagle, she needed to spread her wings and take flight.

The eagle they had been watching flew to a nest, high up on a tree hanging out from the bluff on the other side of the Fox. They could just barely see the heads of two little eaglets waiting for their parent to rip off some of the fish and feed it to them. The mate was setting high up in the top of the tree, watching the activity and guarding the nest.

They had received a tip that a Whiskey Still was being operated in this area and they were taking a drive to see if they could smell anything or see any smoke that would give them a location. The eagles were an unexpected treat.

This was their first trip outside the city and they were amazed at how the scenery had changed so quickly. They had planned to use their sense of smell to spot the odor coming from the Still and their vision to see a trail of smoke. What they were experiencing was so different. They smelled the freshness of the earth not the smoke from the Chicago foundries or the smell from the slaughter houses. Their view of the Fox River and the countryside was pleasant, trees and wild flowers made them forget the city.

Rounding a bend in the road they saw a spot where a buggy or a narrow wheeled wagon had come out of the field and entered the road. The deep tracks in the sod told them it had been loaded heavy. James turned their surrey and followed the tracks into the field. They looked fresh, like they were made last night or early this morning.

After a hundred yards or so of climbing a small hill they could see the tops of a circle of oak trees. Just ahead of them in the road was a gate. It appeared to be the brass head of an old bed. It was wired to wood posts on both ends. The fence was a split rail fence with weeds and brush grown into it so that at spots you could not see the rails. The tracks they were following had gone through the gate. James stopped the surrey and handed Denise the reins. Getting out he took a closer look at the tracks.

"The tracks are coming out," as he straightened he heard the unmistakable sound of a shell being levered into a Henry rifle. Denise heard it to and instinctively her hand went to her hand bag resting on her lap.

"You're trespassing on private property." The raspy voice came from a clump of bushes off to their right.

"Don't do anything rash." James raised his hands shoulder high. "We mean no harm." Turning to face the brush he could see the business end of the rifle.

"Get back in your rig, turn around and get out of here." The grating nasal voice sounded old, tired.

Slowly but surely James climbed back into the surrey. He kept his hands shoulder high so the voice could see them. He did not want to make a sudden move and cause the rifle to spit a slug in their direction. James wanted to get out of this awkward situation, to survive so they could examine what had just happened.

It had been more than a casual property owner stopping someone trespassing. It was more like a man at his post, standing guard. This was not the time to challenge, this was the time to get away and regroup.

Back at the Winton House, after going over the information they had, it was decided they would make a raid. They would do it tomorrow morning at sun rise. The sun would be at their backs giving them better vision than their competition. Early in the morning was a good time to catch them off guard.

It was still dark, just a faint glow of red in the east, as they turned off the dirt road into the field. Now they saw a greater glow of red and yellow ahead of them than to their rear. The brass gate was standing open and a dying fire shown a wavering flicker of flame.

Going through the gate and over the rise they froze in their tracks. In the middle of the stand of oaks was twisted copper and what had once been a still. Fire burned in several places and the stench of burning flesh now reached their nasals.

Mr. Sun was just poking his head up over the lake, it would be an hour before they could see well enough to read the sign of what happened here. It was evident the Whiskey Still had been attacked by a superior force. They would have to accumulate the facts, read the sign of what took place. Make notes so that they did not forget anything of importance. They knew that two people could look at the same thing and both see it different. They would all take notes and compare them later.

"Smithson, ride and get the coroner. Have him bring a wagon to transport these bodies." Wheeler holstered his weapon and took a pencil and note pad from his pocket. "Don't anyone touch a body until the coroner says it is okay."

"Why would anyone do this?" James was looking at an older man, snow white hair and big bushy mustache. He was thinking that it was the raspy voice he had heard coming from the bush.

"I don't know the answer to that but I do know nothing is worth going to Hell for and whoever did this is sure on their way to Hell."

CHAPTER TWENTY

The Chicago White Stocking were having a great barnstorming tour. They had made their way to New Orleans. The crowds had been good and they had won all but a couple of their games. Red was pleased with the condition of the team. A series here in the Big Easy and they would be ready to start league play.

Their hurlers were throwing strikes and the team was hitting well. This was a fun tour for them as the fans in these small towns treated them like heroes. Buying drinks and throwing parties for them. Made them feel like the rich and famous.

Most of the players did not make enough money to not work during the off season. Several had worked as bartenders for McDonald and Big Jim Rasberry had worked as a bouncer. Red would get them to tell stories of working at the Store. Hoping to get some information that they could use.

"McDonald is a good guy to work for but I would hate to have him as an enemy." Rasberry didn't look like an athlete, his body looked like a fifty gallon barrel with arms and legs. He had surprising quickness and sure hands making him a solid infielder.

"Why do you say that?" Red was hoping to get some new information.

"One time we had this guy trying to gamble with fake money, I don't know what happened to him but I saw them take him out of the Store and I never saw him again." Red had to chuckle to himself as he knew how that ended.

"Another time McDonald caught one of his dealers giving winning cards to a friend. I heard they broke the fingers of the dealer and took everything of value from his accomplice and ran them both out of town."

"I have seen McDonald and his wife at parties and they both seem very nice." Red wanted to ask more questions but he hoped this would keep Big Jim talking.

"Like I said, I wouldn't want him for an enemy but he is a good man to have as a friend. He supports the shelter for homeless and runaway kids, he had us taking them food and he would give the older boys work. But he has no time for those women's groups that are anti-liquor or for anyone horning in on his bookmaking territory."

They were in the French Quarter eating Cajun food. Some people think of Cajun food as being extremely spicy and blackened. This couldn't be further from the truth. You could order some dishes that are spicy and some blackened if that is to your taste. The same is true with the ease of eating, it depends on how you order. You can order fried crawfish tails or crawfish boil. Eating the fried tails is much easier and less work than eating the crawfish boil. Few foods make you work for the meat like crawfish.

"Did you go to his bookies and pick up bets?" Red had ordered alligator nuggets, hushpuppies, crawfish cornbread dressing and Brussels sprouts.

"Yes, I made the trip to Gary several times. He would always send at least three of us. One of us stayed with the rig, while the other two went in. There were five different stops in Gary and two of them did a big business." Big Jim had ordered fried crawfish tails, grits, black-eyed peas, and cornbread. Both men were drinking a dark ale with their meal.

The team had won their game that afternoon, they only had a couple more games before heading north. They had one stop on their way to Chicago, Hot Springs Arkansas. They always enjoyed this as the hot springs were becoming famous for healing aches and pains.

"I take it that you think McDonald is a square shooter." Red held up his ale glass as a signal that he needed a refill.

"From what I saw, his games are as fair as they can be. The house always has the advantage so it always wins in the long run. He doesn't have to cheat to win so he doesn't." The waiter came with a pitcher of ale to fill their glasses.

"You going to work for him again this coming off season?" Red had finished his meal, he wiped his mouth with his napkin and placed it on his plate. He pushed back his chair and took a cigar from his inside coat pocket.

"Didn't set anything up for sure. I do not like the Chicago winters, have been thinking of getting something down here. I talked to Casey at the hotel. He said he may have something for me." He took a pipe from his pocket and filled the bowl with tobacco from a pouch. He thumbed a match and put the flame to the bowl.

"I have heard that Casey is so tight he squeezes a dollar until the eagle screams. You sure you want to tie in with him?"

"I have heard that too but it would be just for the off season. I just need something to tide me over and keep me out of the freezing wind coming off Lake Michigan." He puffed his pipe and blew a smoke ring.

"I am buying a billiard and bowling hall, I could use you to help out in the off season."

"Is it down here where it is warm?"

"No, in north Chicago."

"Well like my mother always said when I did something wrong. 'James, you are just like your father'. I think my father would pass up spending another winter in Chicago."

Chapter Twenty-One

Denise was befuddled to say the least. She wanted to do more. She spent most of her time going over notes and reports from agents. She was getting cabin fever. She wanted to get out in the field and do something. They did not allow women to do much but this had never stopped her in the past, why should it now.

Looking over the notes on the wall, it was plain to see that McDonald had broken many laws. They had a great amount of evidence on him but nothing to connect him to murder or the Whiskey Ring. She still felt in her heart that he was the key, that he could solve the mystery of who ordered her father's assassination.

She took a clean sheet of paper and from the wall she listed all the evidence they had on McDonald. She didn't go into detail, just a thumbnail sketch so that McDonald would know she was someone to take serious.

They had his routine. His home address. Even where he went to mass. She wanted to speak to him, one on one, in a public place where he could not exert his power. She had to surprise him, catch him off balance.

A smile came to her face as she remembered one thing that she had that could make the difference. She had not known why she kept it or packed it, but it was time to use it to her advantage. She looked up at the wall again to plan her strategy. She was feeling alive and recharged. She could feel the adrenaline move like a wave through her body.

She had to do this on her own. She could not even tell James what she planned to do. If it backfired it could ruin all the work they had done. Months of putting the pieces of the puzzle together. Was she being selfish? Was she being a poor team player? These questions haunted her as she finished making her list and writing her demand.

She would pray on it, she would ask for guidance. But deep inside she didn't want any guidance that would keep her from doing this.

Denise was still mulling it over in her mind when she crawled between the sheets. She had this ritual she had done ever since her mother had died. She would ask the Lord to bless her and make her do things that her mother would be proud of. In 1875, she added her father. She missed them both and wanted to honor them by doing well. She wondered if what she was doing was for them or for her. She told herself that she didn't want revenge, vengeance. That she didn't want to do harm. She wanted justice. She wanted to do what was necessary in order that the person or persons responsible for her father's death would answer for it.

Sleep didn't come and she was still grasping for an answer when she heard the water wagon roll over the bridge. It was followed by the sound of rain on her window. The water wagon continued to rumble across the night sky and the light show lit up her room. There was something about a thunder storm that calmed her and soon she was sound asleep.

She awoke to the fresh smell of the rain. She liked the smell of the city after a good rain. It tended to wash away the smell of smoke and give the city a new pleasing fragrance. She knew from past experience that it would not last long so she had to enjoy it while she could. Wasn't that the way with so many things in life, you had to enjoy them while you could. She was an idealist. She didn't know for sure where she was going or what she was going to do, but she was on her way.

She had to plan her moves carefully. She wanted to surprise McDonald and keep him off balance. She didn't want him to not know who or what she was. He could not connect her to the Winton House or any federal agency. The less he knew of her the more power she would have over him.

He was a man of power, authority. He was a person who controls, directs and restrains others. It was normal for him to be in charge. She wanted to take him out of his environment, his comfort zone.

She hoped she could make him feel like he had no option but to do what she asked.

How and what she asked was also very important. She could not just ask who ordered the killing of John Fisher in St. Louis. She would have to make it much wider in scope. She could praise his leadership. She could express approval and admiration for his standards of right and wrong. Make that the justification why she didn't just turn him over to the authorities. She had to make him think she needed his ability to think and draw conclusions. It was logical that no one single person knew Chicago better than he did.

If she could get him to believe that by helping her he was helping Chicago. At the same time he was helping himself by keeping some of his activities out of the papers or the hands of the authorities. It could work. She could learn some valuable information that would lead to the person or persons that ordered her father's death.

All the evidence they had collected so far made McDonald out to be a good bad guy, if there was such a thing. She felt the worst thing that could happen was that he would mock her. That he would laugh at this snip of a woman thinking she could challenge him.

She remembered her father telling her to be strong when she felt weak. To be brave when she felt scared and to be humble when she felt victorious. She hoped that she got the opportunity to be humble.

Chapter Twenty-Two

Mike McDonald was at his normal Wednesday table having breakfast. He had a pancake with a sunny side up egg on it, a double order of crisp bacon and black coffee. He had the morning edition of the Chicago Times open to the sports section. This is the way he started each Wednesday and all his friends knew better than to stop at his table to say hello. He did not hear the chair slide on the carpet of the Palmer House dining room or Denise take a seat across the table from him.

When she cleared her throat he put the paper down to see a nun seated at his table. The head waiter now noticed it and stood waiting for McDonald to signal him what if anything to do.

"Mr. McDonald, I need a few minutes of your time. I think you will find it time well spent." Denise held in her hand a large white envelope. "I am sorry to interrupt your breakfast, please continue to eat while I explain my awkward situation."

McDonald did not continue to eat. He put down his fork, closed his newspaper and with a confused look, waited for Denise to continue.

"I have come to the conclusion that you are the only person in Chicago that can help me. The only man with both the power and the interest in Chicago to find an answer for me. I cannot expect you to do this without some benefit so I want you to have this rather than the Chicago Tribune or the federal authorities." Denise placed the envelope on the table and slide it toward McDonald.

He looked at it for a moment before picking it up and taking out the folded sheet of paper. He glanced at it and looked up to meet the eyes of this nun seated across the table from him. He could read nothing in her eyes, her face was expressionless. He dropped his eyes to the paper and continued to read. After several minutes of rereading parts of the paper he folded it and put it back in the envelope.

"You picking a fight with me Sister?"

"No, I was taught never to start a fight, to do everything possible to avoid a fight. But if I found myself in a fight to make sure I won."

"What is it that you want?" He leaned forward over his half eaten breakfast. She had his total attention.

"I want you to use your skill and your organization to find out who is in Chicago that is ordering people killed. Ordering Whiskey Stills to be busted up and people massacred. I know it is not you. That is not your style. But I am sure you know that it is happening. I am not talking about the drunks that shoot it out on Hair-trigger Block. I want the name or names of the people that will stop at nothing to line their pockets."

"What do you plan to do with this information?"

"Give them what they deserve. I don't want good people like yourself to suffer needlessly. The authorities could take down people like yourself and still never get to the real bad apples that will spoil the whole barrel."

"Why did you give me this list?"

"To give you the incentive to help me. You can learn more in a week than the authorities can learn in a year. People will talk to your men."

"Just suppose I do decide to help you. Suppose I come up with a name or names. What then?"

"I will be back in a week to interrupt your breakfast again, you can give me the information. No one needs to know any more than that you are helping out our mission."

Without giving him time to say anything, Denise got up and was gone out the door. McDonald didn't know what to think or do. He looked at his food, it was cold. Just than the waiter came to his table.

"Take this away. Bring me a fresh cup of hot coffee and an apple Danish." He didn't know what had just happened, he had never had anything like this happen to him before. He had to admire the cleverness of this Sister. She was bright, intelligent and had the courage to challenge him to this duel.

He had wondered at many of the things she wanted to know. None of these things had affected him or his operation, so he had given them a pass. Chicago was growing, it was almost a million people and he had told himself that it was just part of the growing pains.

Who could be the muscle behind this? It was time he knew, if not to help out this Catholic Sister, for his own benefit. So far they had been smart enough not to intrude on his operation, but if they continued to grow in power that could change.

He had spent thousands buying protection. He even elected his own mayor. He would put out the word, he would have everyone from the local beat cop to the office of the mayor giving him feedback.

CHAPTER TWENTY-THREE

Johnny boarded the train at the depot in Randalia. He would ride the Rock Island down to Independence where he would get the Illinois Central to Chicago. He carried a cardboard suitcase in one hand and a print flour sack in the other. He did not have many changes of clothes as he did not bring any of his bib-overalls. In the flour sack he had his baseball glove, his shoes with spikes, a pair of wool sweat socks, his baseball bat and an old Randalia baseball uniform.

Johnny wanted to pitch for the Chicago White Stockings. He had just graduated from high school where he had won every game he pitched. Tall and lanky he was a strong farm boy. His hands and fingers were strong from milking cow's morning and night since he was old enough to hold the milk pail between his legs. His arms and shoulders from pitching manure, hay and shoveling snow. Just over six feet and a lean hundred and eighty pounds he looked like an athlete. Even the mop of sandy hair looked active and strong as it didn't seem to belong in any one place.

Johnny got to Lake Front Park just as the White Stockings were taking batting practice before their game. He walked in the player's gate with the visiting team from Cincinnati and being mistaken for one of them, he was not stopped by the guard at the gate. He found his way out on the field and was in awe of his surroundings. He sat his things down by the gate which was just past third base.

Seeing several men standing watching batting practice he made his way toward them. The hitter pulled a foul ball right at Johnny. He reached up with his right hand and caught the ball. Flipped it to his left hand and tossed it to the pitcher in the middle of the diamond. This got the attention of everyone.

"You can't be out here. How did you get past the guard?" The man walking toward him was older, not in very good shape. He was in uniform but Johnny did not think he was a player.

"I came in with the other team. But I would like to pitch for the White Stocking." Johnny got his attention. Players were often enticed to play for other teams if they had not signed a contract.

"Red." He turned back toward the group of men. "You may want to talk to this guy."

Red Foster said something over his shoulder as he walked toward Johnny. He had seen the little effort Johnny had exhibited in fielding the foul ball. It was easy to see he was comfortable on the field.

"I'm Red Foster, the manager. What can I do for you?" He was looking Johnny up and down as he talked.

"I'm Johnny Farmer, and I want to pitch for your team." Johnny didn't know if he should put out his hand, so he did nothing, he just stood there.

"Are you under contract with any team?" Red could see Johnny was not much more than dry behind the ears.

"No sir. I just got out of high school."

"Where you from?"

"Randalia, Iowa. Fred Grant says I am the best that every played there and it maybe a sin but I think he is right."

"Randalia, you say. How big is this Randalia?" Red didn't know if someone was playing a prank on him of if this kid was for real.

"More than a hundred. I know them all but I don't know the exact number."

Red wanted to laugh but he could see that Johnny was serious and there was something about him that he didn't want to embarrass or hurt him. "You're a pitcher? I saw you toss the ball, you're a lefty?"

"Yes, I throw and bat left handed. I play first if I don't pitch. I have played some in the outfield, I run pretty good."

"Well, Johnny you caught us at a bad time, we have to get this batting practice done so Cincinnati can have the field and then we have the game. You can put your things in my office, watch the game and then maybe we can watch you throw some. Dutch will you show him where to put his stuff and find a seat for him to watch the game?"

Dutch nodded his head in agreement and made a motion for Johnny to get his things and follow him. Fans were already starting to fill the seats, some liked to come early and watch batting practice.

The White Stockings beat the Cincinnati team to remain in first place in the National League. They were the defending champions and were off to a very good start this season. But they didn't have a left hand pitcher so it wouldn't hurt to see what this kid had. Red had the catcher stay so he could catch Johnny.

Johnny was wearing his old Randalia uniform and his home made glove. His spikes were old and the toe of the left shoe had a hole in it where he would drag his toe when he threw.

"Just throw me a few straight fast balls to get loose." The catcher took his position behind home plate.

"I really can't throw it straight. It is going to kinda go back to my left or continue on to my right." Johnny stood in the pitcher's box.

"The ump will ask the batter if he wants the pitches to be high or low. If he says low, they have to be from the waist to the knee. If he says high they are from the waist to the letters. Let's say the first batter says he wants them low."

Johnny moved to the back of the pitcher's box. He raised his hands above his head, took a little step, a hop and threw the first pitch on the left edge of the plate knee high. He ended up in the box so it was a good pitch. It looked like it was going to be over the plate but about ten feet from the plate it straightened out and stayed on the outside edge. His next pitch started the same way but this time it continued on across the plate to the inside edge. He threw a half dozen pitches and none of them were over the plate but they were not either outside or inside.

"Can you throw a curve?"

"I throw an eleven/six pitch."

"What's an eleven/six look like?"

Johnny wound up and threw the baseball. It started high, at about eleven on the clock and about ten feet from the plate it dropped to six on the clock about knee high. It was a good thing the catcher was wearing his chest protector has it bounced and hit him in the chest. He turned to look at Red with a look of approval on his face.

"The batter requests high pitches, let's see what you have up there." The catcher took his position and Johnny delivered the first pitch. It was about arm pit high and looked like it would be over the plate but with a screw ball action it straightened out and was on the outside edge. The next pitch was on the inside edge again arm pit high.

"Can you throw harder that this?"

"A little, but I don't have as much control."

"Let's see a high hard one."

Johnny took his wind up and almost jumped at the catcher as he fired the baseball. It was high and hard but right over the plate. Johnny had trouble stopping his forward motion but he stayed in the box. Again the catcher gave Red a look of respect for the young pitcher.

"It's getting late, I will have Dutch take you to the hotel and get you a room. He will talk to them about you eating in the diner. Just sign the meal ticket and put your room number on it. Come back to the park in the morning about nine. We will have you pitch to some batters." Without another word Red turned his back and walked toward his office.

The sun was up in a clear blue sky the next morning when Johnny walked onto the field dressed in his old uniform. One of the guys picked a ball out of a bucket and turning to Johnny asked. "Ya wanta play some catch to warm up?"

"Sure, that would be great." Johnny had his old homemade glove on his right hand. It looked more like a work glove then it did a baseball glove but it would take away some of the sting of the ball. After about ten minutes of tossing the ball back and forth they were interrupted by Red coming on the field.

"Okay, let's see what you got with a batter in the box. Take that bucket of balls and go to the pitcher's box. Goldie, get a stick and take a few cuts." Most of the other players took their positions in the field. Johnny picked up the bucket of balls and went to the center of the diamond.

"Ya want me to let him hit or do you want me to really pitch?" Johnny stood waiting with a ball in his left hand, hanging at his side. "Just throw a few over the plate, let him take a few cuts to start with. Mix them up with high and low pitches." Red stood behind the screen where he could watch.

Johnny pitched one after another over the plate and Goldsmith hit several line drives interspersed with a grounder or pop up. One of the coaches stood behind Johnny catching the balls from the fielders and putting them in the bucket.

"Okay, pitch low and try to keep Goldie from hitting the ball." Red was talking to a man dressed in a suit with a vest and a black string tie.

Johnny's first pitch looked as if it was going to hit the right handed batter but at the last it straightened out and was on the inside edge of the plate. Goldie jumped back before realizing the pitch was in the strike zone. The players in the field gave him some cat calls and he stepped back in, hitting the end of his bat on the plate. Johnny wound up again and this time he threw the ball just above the knees on the outside edge of the plate. Goldie swung and missed. The next pitch he fouled out of play down the first base line. After a daisy cutter of a ground ball and a sky ball to the shortstop, he hit a Texas leaguer over second base.

"Okay, Corcoran. You get in there and take a few cuts. Give him a half dozen pitches to get his stroke before you start throwing hard again." Red motioned for Goldie to come over behind the screen.

"What's he got?"

"Well, he is hard to time. He is not a crafty lefty, he throws hard. Even when he was just throwing it over the plate his pitches are never straight and it is hard to get the fat of the bat of them." Red nodded his head in agreement and motioned for him to go out in the field. Several other batters had about the same success. You could see the respect of the team grow for this lanky young left hander.

"Okay Johnny, that's enough, go out in the garden and shag some balls."

"Garden?" Johnny asked with a puzzled look on his face.

"Outfield. Go to left and send Topp in to hit." Johnny showed them that he could cover some ground and catch the ball. So far this young man was proving to be all that he said he was. After they had all taken their cuts at the plate it was Johnny's turn. Again they were pleased with what they saw. He had some pop in his bat and the ball tended to jump off it. He demonstrated power to all fields and was able to pull several pitches over the short right field fence.

"We need to get his kid under contract before some other team learns how good he could be." Red saw one of the local reporters making notes. "We have to keep him away from the reporters until we get him signed." The man in the business suit nodded his head in agreement.

"Johnny, will you go with Mr. Spalding, he will talk to you about being a member of the Chicago White Stockings, have you sign some papers."*

*In 1889 the Chicago White Stockings nickname became the "Colts" as they had such a young team and then it was changed to the Chicago Cubs.

Chapter Twenty-four

Mike McDonald was at his table in the Palmer House but he only had a cup of coffee in front of him. He didn't even have his morning paper. He was waiting for this mystery Catholic Sister to show up. He put his people to work and they had come up with an accumulation of facts. He was surprised himself at some of the knowledge he had learned about Chicago. Knowledge is good, but it is wisdom that is the ability to judge which aspects of the knowledge are applicable to the problem.

One thing his people struck out on was in finding out anything about this Sister. She was not from any of the churches, missions, or orphanages. It was as if she did not have any actual existence. No one in Chicago had ever seen or heard of her. It was as if she were a ghost.

McDonald could not remember when he was more anxious to see someone. He did not sleep well last night thinking about this meeting. He wanted same reassurance that she had been real. That she had not been just a figment of his imagination.

When he saw her come in the dining room he gave out a huge sigh of relief. He stood with a smile from ear to ear and made a gesture for her to have a seat. Denise did not know what to expect, but this welcome was not one of the things that had crossed her mind.

"Before we get to our business, I would like for you to join me for breakfast." He motioned for the waiter.

"Oh, no I...." He interrupted, "Please it would be my pleasure to dine with you." He handed her a menu as he spoke.

She did not plan on this. She had hoped to get her information and be gone. She was pushing her luck. It was not common for one nun to be alone in public. It would draw attention. She had been lucky the first meeting and she had hoped to be in and out this time before it became a problem.

"Mr. McDonald it would not be proper for me to dine with you in public, I hope you understand."

"I do. There is a small private dining room, right here. Would that be to your satisfaction?" With his finger he pointed to a door just a few feet away.

"That would be much better and I could join you for some coffee while we talked."

Without saying a word he got to his feet and went to the door. He opened it and held it for her to enter. It was small with an oak table and six oak chairs. A chandelier hung from the ceiling over the center of the table. A big window provided the small room with more than adequate light. A waiter placed a large tray on the table. A coffee pot, cream, and sugar. McDonald poured them each a cup of steaming hot coffee.

"Do you take sugar or cream in your coffee?"

"No, thank you, this is fine." She took a sip of her coffee, not knowing just where to start.

"I found out a great deal that I was not aware of." He placed a white envelope on the table. "But there was one thing I could not learn anything about?"

"What was that?" She took another sip of her coffee, it was so hot she had to be careful. "Who you are and where you came from. You are not with any of the Chicago churches, missions or orphanages." He took a sip of his coffee and waited for an explanation.

"Is that of importance?"

"I like to know who I am dealing with and what their motivation might be. So, yes it is of importance."

"I guess you would say I was a rogue from a convent in St. Louis. I do not represent anyone but myself." She could feel her face flush.

"St. Louis. Why is a Catholic Sister from St. Louis interested in Chicago?" He held his cup with both hands near his mouth. He blew on the edge of the cup before he took a sip. All the time keeping his eyes on those of Denise.

She put down her cup as she took a large deep breath. She had the realization that it was time for her to tell the truth. Anything but the truth would only cause difficulty. Well, maybe not the whole truth, just the part of how she became a nun.

"My mother died when I was very young and my father raised me. I was with him in St. Louis. It was 1875 and he made me promise that if he did not come back to the hotel that I would go to the convent and I would stay there until I was at least twenty. Later I learned that he had been shot. I did some investigating in St. Louis and learned that the order to have him killed came from Chicago. To be honest, I thought it came from you. I have sense learned that you do not operate that way. I thought I could use your power and organization to find out who ordered my father's death."

"You are one resourceful Sister to say the least." He sipped his coffee. "I like quick-witted people, people that are good at thinking of ways to get things done."

"You are not angry with me?"

"No, in fact I should thank you for bringing some of this to my attention. I was treating Chicago like it was six or seven years ago and it has grown greatly. With this growth have come some people that are not good for Chicago and what is not good for Chicago is not good for me."

"Were your people able to find out anything?"

"Yes, but not enough to prove it in a court of law. I feel I know as you say, who the rotten apples are." He pushed the white envelope over to Denise.

She picked it up and paused before opening it.

"Layla Mae Wilcox?"

"Yes, she is the brains and she is ruthless. She has no pity, she is cruel and shows no mercy." He took the coffee pot and refilled his cup, he reached to give Denise some but she held up her hand.

"Who is she? Why would she order my father's death?" Denise asked in a puzzled tone of voice.

"She and her husband have the Dixie Distillery and they have their fingers into counterfeit Oleo and a protection racket in Haymarket. They were cheating on their federal liquor taxes and your father got too close to a man that could connect them to the swindle."

Denise was dazed, confused. She stared at her coffee cup with a bewildered look on her face.

"They came up from the south near the end of the Civil War. They got a start here and have built up a powerful operation. I had no idea that they were mixed up in all the under hand things that they are." McDonald leaned back in his chair and sipped his coffee.

"You seem confident of what you say, but you say you have nothing that will stand up in a court of law?" Denise warmed her hands on her coffee cup, suddenly she was cold. She did not know what to expect, but she did not expect such a detailed account.

"No, none of this can be proved to a judge but I feel confident that what I have told you is the truth. What do you plan to do with this information?"

"I do not know. I ...."

"May I make a suggestion?" He said interrupting her.

"Yes, of course."

"I suggest that you go back to your St. Louis convent, your work here is done. Get a Chicago paper to read each morning after your morning prayers. Let nature take its course."

Denise could not help but wonder what the little smile on his face meant. She did not know what to say or do so she just sipped her coffee.

"May I ask you a question, Sister?"

"Of course."

"Let's just say if it had been me and that I was so confident of myself and my power over a Sister that I just bragged about being the one that ordered your father's death. What would you have done?" He sipped his coffee as he waited for her answer. "We never know what we will do in a situation like that but I can tell you what I had planned to do. I had planned to reach into my bag and have Mr. Remington talk for me." She patted her hand bag.

"A Sister with a gun? You continue to be full of surprises. Do you really believe that you could shoot someone?"

"I don't know and I hope and pray that I never find out. My father taught me to shoot, so the mechanical part would not be a problem."

"You have done all that you need to do. You have given Chicago all the information it needs. Chicago wants to thank you for bringing this to their attention and I feel confident that Chicago will deal out justice. We both know that nothing can bring back your father but I feel sure that he is very proud of you. First for doing what he asked you to do and second for not letting this go." McDonald stood up and extended his hand to Denise.

She took his hand and thought how things had turned out. She was sure Red Foster had killed her father. When he turned out to be a friend, she was sure McDonald had ordered it. Now that turns out to be false and she looks at McDonald as a friend. She picked up the paper, placed it in the envelope and walked out. She hailed a cab and told the driver to take her to the train station.

At the Union Station she walked up to the ticket window, talked to the agent. After a minute or two she turned and walked into the restroom. In a few minutes, Denise walked out dressed in her street clothes. She went outside, hailed a cab and went to the Brown Hotel. Inside she took a seat in the lobby and watched the door to see if she were followed. A few minutes later, she went out the back door and walked to the Winton House.

CHAPTER TWENTY-FIVE

"WHAT THE HELL YOU MEAN SHE JUST DISAPPEARED?"
McDonald was seated behind his big oak desk, in his office at the
Store. He stood as he stared fiercely at the small man standing in
front of his desk.

"I followed her as you told me to do. She caught a cab to the Union
Station." He spoke filled with fright. "She went to the ticket window
and then into the ladies room. I waited and she never came out. After
about twenty minutes I asked Helen at the lunch counter to check for
me. She was not in there. There was no sign of her." His fear was so
great that he could not stand still, he rocked back and forth.

McDonald nodded his head and sat back down. "I should not be
angry with you, she fooled me too. She is clever, thinks ahead and is
prepared to handle whatever comes up." He made a motion with his
hand for the man to leave and he was more than happy to do just that.
He hurried out of the office, closing the door behind him.

At the Winton House, Denise was not prepared for whatever came up.
She did not have a clue as to how she could use the information that
she had. She did not want to lie about how she got the information.
She did not want to tell them what she had done. She was looking
at all the notes on the wall. The chart she had made. The note from
Red Foster caught her eye. This could be a way.

Red had said that the man asked about Lila Mae Lewis. That she
was strikingly beautiful and as ruthless as she was pretty. That she
came from a whiskey making family and had gone to Chicago after
having a problem with Confederate Soldiers where one was killed at
her distillery. Lila Mae Lewis, Layla Mae Wilcox. They had to be
one and the same. There was another note that James had posted.

Mrs. Wilcox according to her driver: "What's on the inside is
different than what you see on the outside. She is the boss, she runs

the company. She tells him what to do and what not to do. He gives all the orders but they come from her. She knows her whiskey, she is very shrewd."

She also found her note, the comment Mrs. Wilcox had made about Haymarket. Things were beginning to add up. She could bring all this to Mr. Wheeler's attention. They could swing their investigation from McDonald to the Wilcox.

She was happy with her findings. The smile on her face showed the pleasure she felt inside.

"What you look so pleased about?" James came in from the stable where he and Mose had been working on the equipment.

"I think I have come up with something. McDonald is turning out to be a dead end. Oh, he is breaking and bending the law but what you found out at that still is not his style at all. But I think I have found someone that fits the villain role."

"Who would that be?" James came over to where she was at the wall.

"Look at all these notes. Each by itself is not impressive but when you consider them all together. When you eliminate McDonald. They tend to paint a picture of a very sinister lady."

"Yes, I do see a pattern. You could be on to something. Be interesting to hear what Wheeler has to say about it." James was going over the notes a second time. "I don't see anything that would connect them to your father's murder."

"No. The only thing is they do run a distillery and could have been mixed up with the Whiskey Ring." Denise had to bite her lip, she did not like playing this game with James. He did not deserve it. She would have to find a way and a time to tell him the truth. She knew the longer she waited the more he would be hurt by her deceit.

"If we rule McDonald out and I think we have. The Wilcox would be as good candidates as any I know." James turned to leave.

"James?"

"Yes."

"May we go for a walk? I have some things that I need and want to tell you."

"Sure, let me just go tell Mose." He went out the back door to the stable. In just minutes he was back and the two of them walked down toward the lake. It was a nice day for a walk, the clear bright cloudless sky made Lake Michigan shine like a mirror.

Denise started to speak several times, getting out only a word or two of confused attempts to start a conversation. James let her suffer, it was not often that she was not in control. It was he who had been in this situation many times, he rather enjoyed seeing Denise a little speechless.

"I don't…. I do…." Denise just didn't seem to be able to get started.

"Would it help you if I told you that I saw you sneak out a week ago and again this morning in your habit?" James did not turn to look at her, he preferred to imagine the look on her face.

"You saw me? You saw me and didn't ask any questions?" "I figured if you wanted me to know, you would tell me." He was rather enjoying this.

"You didn't follow me? You were not even curious as to what I was doing or where I was going?"

"Yes, I was very curious, but I felt you were safe dressed in your habit and when you came back and didn't say anything I felt you wanted to keep it a secret." This time he did turn to look at her and saw that she was more angry than embarrassed. He knew what was happening, she was turning this around to make it his fault. If leather were brains, he wouldn't have enough to saddle a bed bug when it came to her.

CHAPTER TWENTY-SIX

Johnny had a loft apartment over Red's Billiards and Bowling Hall. Looking out his east window he could see Lake Michigan. It was not far from Lake Front Park and it had a lunch counter. They did not have a large menu. They served Red Hot's, a sausage on sweet flat bread with mustard, pickled eggs, cheese with hardtack and Oxtail soup. The soup was something Red had found on one of his spring baseball trips down south. It was a tomato base with Oxtail, potatoes, chopped onions, carrots and celery.

The Oxtail tail was cow or bull tails that he could buy at any of the packing plants. They got them fresh, skinned them and prepared them with a special mixture of herbs and spices. Red gave a Cajun Chef in Baton Rouge an autographed baseball for the secret recipe. The soup was a favorite of Chicago. After mid-night it was not uncommon to see a table dressed in evening clothes dining next to a table of fishermen. Eating and having a night cap.

Chicago being so near Wisconsin it was easy to obtain some very good cheese. They served everything from goat cheese to Limburger with a very good Swiss cheese being the most popular.

Johnny liked being close to the food and bar. The experience of living in downtown Chicago. He liked to watch them bowl and play billiards. He had shot pool, eight ball and rotation but had never seen a billiards table. They did have some pocket type pool tables and from time to time, Johnny would play. Fred Grant had taught him how to control the cue ball with English and play position so he could more than hold his own. Johnny had never dreamed that signing with the Chicago White Stockings could change his life so much. He was not prepared for it. He had more money than he ever dreamed of having. He had signed for seventy-five dollars a month plus expenses while on the road. They had given him fifty dollars just to sign so that he had money until his first monthly check. This was something he had dreamed about ever since he was knee high to a grasshopper.

The team was doing very well. Red drilled fundamentals, they all had something to do on each batted ball. He taught a coordinated effort to back each other up, to hit the cutoff man with throws from the outfield and be aggressive on the bases. They had sliding practice and Red was a master at the hook slide.

The White Stockings used hand signals to tell the batter and base runners what to do. Most of the other teams in the league didn't even know they were using them. Red could call the suicide squeeze or hit and run from the bench. There was only one umpire so Red taught them how to watch the ump and if he was looking toward first or second where there may be a play, the runner could cut third. Not run all the way to third base, just cut the corner short and head for home.

Red had a big sign in the locker room. The four "B's of baseball. Brains, brawn, bravery, and bluster. He wanted the team to be proud. To go on and off the field with an air of confidence. He wanted them to expect to win and to do the little things that were necessary to win. He wanted them to dress sharp so he made a deal with a large men's clothing store to fix them up. In return the players had to take their turn being at the store to sign autographs.

Red was doing very well so he talked Albert Spalding into selling him twelve percent of the team for three thousand, seven hundred and fifty dollars. He had a good man running his billiards and bowling and being that several of the players lived there and were often downstairs helped to bring in customers. If a Chicagoan could go to work saying that he beat Johnny Farmer in a game of pool, it was better than any advertising he could buy. Johnny would write to his grandparents, who had raised him and send them money. They lived on a small farm just outside Randalia. They were very proud of him but worried about him in the big city. He would send them clippings from the Chicago papers that had his name in them.

He was not getting to pitch much as the team had their rotation. But he was playing some outfield and once in a while Red would let him play first base. Red had told him to be patient that if one of the guys in the rotation got hurt, he would step in to take his place.

Johnny liked to walk down to the pier and watch the sailboats. He had never seen anything like them. He still did not understand how they could sail against the wind. It was a time he treasured. A time he could relax and get away from the crowds.

It was one of these evenings that he met Leah. She was sailing a small sailboat back and forth in beautiful Belmont Harbor. Johnny sat on the pier watching her zig zag when going to the north which was against the wind. He thought the arm of the sail was going to knock her out of the boat but she always ducked at the last minute and let it swing past.

"Ahoy." She shouted. "Can you grab my line if I toss it to you?" Even at this distance Johnny could see her bright blue eyes wide with confidence and determination. She was wearing a sailor dress and hat that made it hard to guess her age. But there was no mistaking her sweetness. Even in the twilight of the evening, Johnny could see those qualities. "I will do my best." Johnny stood and walked to the edge of the pier toward her dinghy. She tossed him a coiled rope that would have hit him in the chest had he not caught it. When he didn't do anything she flashed a smile, showing pretty white teeth and a sense of amusement.

"Just pull the dinghy in and tender it to the pier." Johnny pulled the rope hand over hand and the small sailboat came up to the pier. Johnny watched this tall, slender, quick and sure-footed beauty step out of the moving boat onto the pier, he seemed to be in a daze.

She took the rope from him and bending down she did a figure eight around the horn cleat to secure the boat to the dock. She did the same to the stern to keep it from swinging out.

"I see you here often, do you sail?"

"No. I just like to watch the boats."

"My name is Leah, what do they call you?" She held out her hand toward him.

"Johnny." He took her hand and was surprised by the firmness of her grip. She had taken him by surprise, he didn't know what to say or do. He thought she must be a year or two younger than he was but it was difficult to tell. She was so sure of herself, so comfortable.

"Would you like to sail with me up to my place, I have to be home before it gets dark?"

"No. No thanks. But, thanks for asking." Johnny again was surprised by her even asking. He was caught off guard. Randalia had not prepared him for anything like this. The smile on her face indicated she knew he would decline her invitation.

"We are having a cookout tomorrow night, Southern style. Just up the lake, 852 Lake Shore. Come anytime, we will start eating about seven.

It is be casual, what you're wearing would be fine." Before Johnny could reply she got into her boat and adjusted the sail. She pointed to the horn cleats and Johnny unwrapped the ropes and tossed them in the boat.

He watched as she sailed north into the slight breeze. She used a zig zag pattern until she got around the bend and then she sailed to the west out of his line of sight.

That night Johnny went to slept with a vision of Leah in his head. Those big blue eyes, dark hair and the willowy quickness of her young body were etched into his memory.

CHAPTER TWENTY-SEVEN

The Chicago team was leading the St. Louis Brown Stockings four to three in the sixth inning when the big left handed first baseman hit a sharp line drive back through the pitcher's box. The hurler, Teagarden, reached for it more from reflex than intention, and the hard smash hit his pitching hand. The ball glanced off to the third baseman but he did not have a play on the speedy runner.

Red, playing first base, called time and went to Teagarden who was bend over in pain. His hand was already swelling, he would not be able to continue. Red helped him to the sideline and called to Johnny.

"Farmer! You got the ball. Get loose." Red motioned for the club house man to come. "Get some ice on this and have Doc take a look at it." He turned and went to the umpire to report the change of pitchers.

Johnny pitched well, the Brown's only got two hits and didn't score in the four innings he worked. He helped his own cause with a sharp line drive to right field that bounced over the fence for a ground rule double.

After the game Johnny felt good about how he had played. He got cleaned up and thought he would take Leah up on her invitation. He walked up Lake Shore, all the homes were huge with high stone fences. He was still half a block from 852 when he heard the music. There was a Negro man at the gate. He took one look at Johnny and with a smile from ear to ear waved him in.

"Youse guts to be the Johnny Miss Leah asked me to look out for. Just follow you nose." He pointed up the hill toward the sound of the music.

When Johnny got to the top of the incline he saw a large home with a lawn full of tables with white cloths, a band playing and at least a hundred people milling around with drinks in their hands. Lanterns were hung on poles all over the yard. It was not what he had expected. He spotted Leah talking and laughing with some young people down toward the boat house. Dressed in a long white dress he thought she looked angelic.

His mind told him it was uncomfortable and wanted to get out of here but his legs kept walking toward Leah. He was half way down the slope when she saw him and came running. His brain said it was too late now, he was just going to have to suffer through this.

"Johnny, you came. I was afraid that you wouldn't." She came to him and took his hand. Her hair had a shine almost as bright as her eyes.

"Hey, you didn't tell me you were Johnny the baseball star."

"You didn't tell me you were Leah the heiress." He made a sweeping motion with his hand toward the tables and band.

"Oh, that's nothing. Don't worry about it. I want you to meet some of my friends." She pulled him toward the boathouse and the group she had been talking with. She was halfway through the introductions when they were called to come eat.

There were three long tables full of food and people going down both sides filling their plates. Johnny watched Leah and made an attempt to do as she did. They got their food and went to one of the open tables to eat with some of Leah's friends.

"You get enough to eat?" Leah asked as she looked at his clean plate.

"I'm full as a tick." He patted his stomach with both hands and leaned back in his chair.

The night was a series of new experiences for Johnny. He was introduced to so many new things and people. He played croquet. This game where you hit this wooden ball through these hoops they called wickets. A game of skill and strategy where the players were fiercely competitive. He danced to what they called the Virginia reel. A dance where two lines of partners perform a number of different dance steps. He ate okra and potatoes with bacon and cheese all mixed together, sautéed beet greens, lima beans, deviled eggs, fried chicken and something they called mince pie. He passed on the roasted Pidgeon's and the stewed duck. He drank cherry punch and even signed a few autographs.

Back in his room he had trouble turning his mind off and going to sleep. It had been a great day, the game had gone well, the party was fun and he had not embarrassed himself. He felt so comfortable around Leah. He never would have been able to handle that party without her helping him at every turn. When he finally did fall asleep he slept hard as he was exhausted.

The next morning he slept late, had a quick breakfast at the lunch counter and was on his way to the ball park when he was approached by a man.

"You Johnny Farmer?" The man was tall, taller than Johnny. He was dressed in a fancy suit and had a derby with a rounded crown and narrow brim covering his very blond hair.

"Yes, I am. What can I do for you?" Johnny was being noticed more and more on the streets, he thought this was just another fan.

"I have a message for you." His tone of voice had changed. His jaw was set and his eyes narrowed as he looked down into Johnny's. "You stay away from Leah Wilcox or I'll break your arm in so many pieces you won't even be able to pitch pennies."

CHAPTER TWENTY-EIGHT

They were all at the big oak table in the Winton House. They had papers and tin-types spread all over the table. They were planning a new strategy now that they had eliminated McDonald from the killing in Missouri. They had a new target but no hard evidence that pointed to the Wilcox. All they had was what McDonald had told Denise. The question they had to answer was, did he do this to send them on a wild goose chase or was he being honest with the Catholic Nun. Had he figured out who Denise was? Did he know she was living at the Winton House and was not a member of the convent in St. Louis?

"The first thing we have to do is figure out how much we trust McDonald." Paul Wheeler got to his feet to refill his coffee cup.

"I know I shouldn't have done this on my own. I am sorry that I didn't get your permission. I…."

"What's done is done. We have gone over that, we have to move on." Wheeler returned to the table sipping on his fresh, hot coffee. "We need to get someone inside the Wilcox organization. James do you know anything about making whiskey?"

"No, I don't even know anything about drinking it. But I do know a little about making barrels. I helped my father make some."

"That's a skill not too many Chicagoan's have. Go down to the Dixie Distillery and see if they could use another barrel maker. Denise, you are not to leave the house. I don't want you outside, not even to go to church. If McDonald doesn't know who and what you are we cannot take the chance of him finding out. If he does know, I don't want you someplace his men could grab you. I want you to get a report ready to send to Washington. You can tell them what we learned from McDonald but not your part in finding it out. Mose, I want you to take Milly to the market, get with the other drivers. See if you can learn anything. Wolfgram, you have Anderson help Denise with the reports and you go to the drop point and see if Red has anything for us. Smithson go check with your people to see if they have anything. Tell them the new target." He got to his feet indicating the meeting was over and expecting them to all do their assignments without any further explanations.

James went to find some work clothes. He had to go see if he could get a job making barrels. He was trying to remember all that his father had taught him about barrel making. They had made a few out of pine to hold flour and grain. The one's to hold liquid were made out of oak or chestnut.

Cooper, that's what he was trying to remember. A barrel maker was called a Cooper. He would ask for a job as a Cooper, this would at least get him started on the right foot. There was a huge demand for barrels in Chicago with all the packing plants, breweries, and distilleries. Some of the barrels were emptied and could be reused rather quickly but those of the distilleries had to age for years. A good many were shipped out of the city, never to return.

There was a line of men waiting at the distillery to apply for a job. Chicago was growing daily and all those coming to the city were looking for work. After a wait of about a half hour James made it to the table just inside the door.

"Like to get a job as a Cooper." He told the man behind the long table. He looked up at James with a surprised look on his red face. He looked Irish and he looked like a boozer, his red nose showed the blood vessels.

"You got any experience making barrels?" His eyes were running up and down James.

"Yes sir, both wet and dry." James was trying his best to give the man an idea that he was who he said he was, without bragging or without giving too much information.

"Let me see those paws."

James held out his hands and the man ran his fingers over the palms, it had been awhile since James had done any real hard work but the callous were still there.

"Go over to that table on the right and Linda will get your information. You report to work in the morning at seven sharp."

"Thank you." James got to his feet and went to the table on the right. Most of the other men were going to a table on the left where there was a waiting line. There was no one waiting at the table on the right.

"Have a seat. Do you read and write?" Linda was a large woman of middle age. She too, looked to be Irish. Her hair was not red but it had a red tint to it. She had freckles on her arms and a couple of small light-brown spots on her nose.

"Yes, I do both." James took a seat at the table.

She handed James a paper and pencil. "Fill this out. Your pay will be sixteen dollars a week and you will work sixty hours."

James took the paper and pencil and stated to fill out the form. They had an address at a flop house so that he didn't have to give the Winton House address.

"No drinking on the job, don't be late to work and don't come hungover." She was watching as he put in his information.

"Where do I report for work?" It was not a long form and did not take James long to fill out his basic information.

"Today is Wednesday. You won't get paid this Saturday. Next Saturday you will be paid twenty-four dollars if you do your job. When you are done here, Randy will show you where to be at seven in the morning." She nodded toward a man leaning against the door jam.

Randy looked to be Scandinavian, tall with almost white blond hair and blue eyes. He shrugged his broad shoulders and ran his hand through his hair as he nodded to James.

"Follow me and I will show you where we make our barrels," he had a strong Swedish accent. "It is one of the best places to work. The foreman, Glenn Andersen is remarkable. He knows his stuff and is one of the most cheerful guys I know. Always smiling. Always laughing. Just don't show up late or be careless with your work. He won't put up with a slacker but do a good job and he will walk the river with you."

CHAPTER TWENTY-NINE

Johnny was doing his best to get comfortable in the sleeper. They were on their way to play the Philadelphia Centennials and then to New York to play the Mutualist. It was his first time in a Pullman where the velvet seat folded down into a bed. The curtain hung down and helped but he was still uneasy.

All at once the curtain was swept aside and a man was in his face. It was the same man that approached him on the way to the ballpark.

"Farmer, are you hard of hearing or just plain stupid? I told you to stay away from that girl. Now you will wish that you had." He had a blackjack in his hand and he raised it to hit Johnny.

Johnny turned on his side and as he did he hit the man on the side of his head with his baseball bat. The man fell to the floor, making enough noise to get everyone's attention. Goldie was the first one there but in just minutes the whole team was wanting to know what happened.

Red got everyone back to their sleepers. The porter returned with the Railroad Marshal.

"What's going on here?" The marshal looked to be too young for his position. He was tall and thin, couldn't be much older than Johnny.

"This guy attempted to assault one of my players, keep him on ice for a few days." Red was helping the stunned man to his feet. Blood was running down his face from a cut on his cheek bone.

"What's that on the floor?" The marshal took the man from Red and put him in cuffs helping him to stand as his legs were jelly.

Red picked up the blackjack and handed it to the marshal. "He was going to use this on my player. I will sign papers to press charges later if you need me to."

The marshal, half dragging the staggering man went out of the Pullman car.

"What's this all about?" Red asked Johnny.

Johnny told him of the man approaching him on the way to the park and that Leah Wilcox was waiting after the game and gave him a lift to the train station. When Red heard the girl's name his interest increased.

"He was about to hit me with that thing when I smacked him with Old Bessie." Johnny was still in his sleeper, covered with a blanket.

"Old Bessie?"

Johnny held up his bat. "Bessie Jellings gave me the white ash to make her so I call her Old Bessie. I always sleep with her by my side."

"Let's keep that between the two of us. Don't tell the players or the reporters anything about Old Bessie. If anyone asks just tell them you hit him with a left hook."

"But that would be a lie!"

"Sometimes Johnny it is better to tell a little white lie then to tell the whole truth. If you tell anyone about Old Bessie it will spread like wild fire. The fans and the opponents will be all over it and you will never hear the end of it. Now you try to get some sleep and if you need to talk about it we can do that in the morning." Red closed the curtain and went back to his sleeper. Johnny had a difficult time drifting off to sleep but the rocking of the train soon had him in a deep sleep.

The team played well in Philadelphia, Johnny pitched the third game of the series and held the Centennials to just four hits winning four to one. It was a little different playing on the road, he did not get the called strikes that he got in Chicago. He had to make his pitches better but Red had prepared him. Johnny had a way of making his pitches look like they would be easy to hit and most of the players could not lay off them.

Leah had asked him to write to her so he sent her a short note on the hotel stationary. He didn't tell her anything about the incident on the train. He thought it better that he not say anything rather than to lie about what happened.

In New York it rained the first day so they had to play a double header the last day of the series. Johnny pitched the second game of the twin bill, gave up only two runs and hit a three run homer to give the White Stockings a five to two win. He was fast becoming a player reporters liked to write about. The farmer from Iowa, the farmer boy, farmer throws a hayseed, this southpaw right out of high school, were just a few of the phases used in the papers.

Johnny had to admit that he liked to read his name in the papers and he cut out the clippings to keep or send to his grandparents. It was still very hard for him to believe that he was playing baseball in New York City and getting paid to do it. Just months ago he was in his room on the farm dreaming about it.

The train ride back to Chicago was long but it was uneventful for Johnny. When they pulled into the station in Chicago a large group of fans were on hand to welcome them back from their successful road trip. One of these fans was Leah Wilcox.

"Johnny!" She waved to him from the edge of the crowd. He took his bags and made his way to her.

"Johnny, come I have my surrey. I can give you a lift to your place." She was dressed in a blue jumper that made her eyes bluer and her hair darker. She took his elbow and led him to her surrey. The driver helped Johnny with his bags and helped Leah into the surrey. He gave Johnny a suspicious look that Johnny could not mistake.

"I was told not to go anywhere near you." The driver spoke to his horse and they headed up the street toward the Billiards and Bowling

Hall where Johnny roomed. "I don't think your parents approve of me."

"I know. I had a huge argument with my mother. She thinks now that you are becoming more famous the papers will pick up on us and it will embarrass the family. I think it is awesome and I told her that I was going to the station to meet you. I am sure my driver is to report everything as soon as I get back to the house." She squeezed his arm and giggled.

"I don't want to cause any trouble for you with your parents."

"Oh, it's okay. I think dad is fine with it. It is just mother, she thinks I should only talk with who she calls the right people."

"You like me because I play baseball?" The driver stopped the surrey in front of Red's B & B.

"Johnny, I didn't know you were a ball player when I docked my boat and asked you to the cookout." She let go of his arm and turned to face him. "In fact I wish you weren't a baseball player. I don't like you going on these road trips and all these girls flirting with you."

CHAPTER THIRTY

It didn't take them long to realize that James was too valuable a man to have just cutting the top grove in a barrel for the head to fit into. He was promoted to foreman where he walked up and down the line as the barrels were made checking on each man's work. He did this in such a way as to make the men want to do their best work. He did not cuss and swear like the man that had the position before him. He did not call the workers names, he just helped them to make the best barrels the fastest. Their production went up and the quality of work was noted.

At this new position he had time to look around and see the whole operation. He got to go in the office each night to give them the barrel count and he made friends with one of the women that worked there. He did not see Mrs. Wilcox but Mr. Wilcox was in and out of the office each day.

He listened to the talk and asked questions but learned very little of value. One evening while posting the barrel count for the day he heard talk coming from one of the offices.

"There's a new Whiskey Still working down near the stock yards, they sold some product to one of my regular customers. Cost me a sale." James could not see the man, the door was only open a crack.

"I'll report it to Wilcox, see how he wants to handle it. You find out as much information about it as you can."

James heard someone walk toward the door so he quickly turned his back and walked toward the outer door. He just had his hand on the door knob when the man came out. He didn't turn to look or give any indication that he even knew he was there. The man didn't say anything so he just opened the door and went out.

At the Winston House he told Denise what he had learned. She wrote it up, dated it and posted it on the wall with the other notes they had. She was getting cabin fever, she had hardly been out of the house. She liked her work but she missed her church, she missed walking down to the lake and going to the market.

"I have to speak to Wheeler. I need a change of routine. I feel like I am in a prison." She stepped back to look at the board. It contained notes on everything that pertained to the Wilcox. Red had reported the incident on the train and she had that on the board. James put his hand on her shoulder from behind.

"I know this has been very difficult for you. We have not heard anything but that McDonald thinks this nun went back to St. Louis. I think if he were to talk to you face to face he would know your voice and recognize your eyes. But from a distance I don't think he would connect you with the nun." She put her hand over his and backed up so that it was almost as if his arm was around her.

"Thanks. It helps that you understand." They were standing like that when Wheeler entered the room from the back.

"Anything new?"

They moved apart quickly and Denise showed him the note on what James had overheard. He thought about it for a moment before speaking.

"We need to find the location if possible and watch it. We could get lucky and catch them in the act. It appears they do not like any competition. They were not opposed to using strong arm tactics against the baseball player their daughter is interested in. I have a man keeping an eye on him. We don't know if the guy from the train is back in town or if they still have him on ice in Pennsylvania"

"I need to talk to you about changing my routine. I am starting to get cabin fever." Denise turned to face Wheeler.

"Well that may not be a problem. Washington is getting some requests from the officials in Colorado to open an office there. Colorado is going through some growing pains and the local law enforcement has asked for federal help."

"What does that have to do with me and my routine?"

"They asked me if I thought you two were ready to open the office out there and set things up."

James and Denise could not believe what they were hearing. They had never dreamed of going back to Colorado as federal agents. They did enjoy what they were doing and they had got praise from Wheeler and from Washington but this was something else.

"I can't go anywhere until I know who ordered my father's death. McDonald said it was the Wilcox but I can't leave Chicago with them still living in that big house free as birds."

"Well, it is still in the talking stage. Washington just wanted my opinion. Nothing may happen, the wheels turn slow in Washington but they do like your work and this seemed like a good time to give you guys a heads up. I think it would be fine for you to go about your business in the city. Just do your best not to come face to face with McDonald."

Wheeler went back to his office and Denise looked at James who looked bewildered to say the least.

"What do you make of that?" Her question made him snap back to the here and now.

"It never dawned on me that we may do this for a life time. I always assumed that once we found out the truth about your father's death it would be over. That you would go back to the mission and I would go back to the valley. I have come to like life in the city and don't think I would be happy back in Eagle Valley but living a life as a federal agent never crossed my mind. What about you?"

"Like Paul said, nothing may happen, the wheels turn slow in Washington but I am glad that they like our work. It is always nice to be appreciated. I am also relieved that I can get out, I will go to church and pray on it. It is nice to be empowered with a choice."

James thought how easy it had been when they had a purpose. Making changes can be bewildering, frightening and even depressing. He felt things would sort themselves out. He remembered the French saying he had heard Mose say, "Advienne que pourra, come what may."

CHAPTER THIRTY-ONE

The White Stockings won their first game of the home stand. Johnny played in the outfield and went two for three at the plate. He hit a double that drove in two of the four runs the team needed to win. He came out of the club house to a group of fans waiting for an autograph. He signed several, many with a stub of a lead pencil while walking with his head down, asking what name to put on it. When he got a surprise.

"My dearest Leah, would be great." The smile and giggle just made him melt with embarrassment. But he recovered in time to write.

When she saw what he had wrote, she hit him on his shoulder.

"Don't you be mean to me, it's not you. When you're done here, come over to my surrey." She skipped away before he could respond.

Johnny signed several more autographs and then walked over to her surrey where she and her driver were waiting. He had never really had a girlfriend in Randalia. His life had been school, baseball and working on his grandparents farm. Randalia was a great place to grow up but it did not prepare him for Leah. He knew Leah was way out of his league but he couldn't help but like her. She made him feel so charged with energy when he was with her. It was much like the feeling he got when he hit the ball well or struck out a good hitter.

"You sure are popular. I hear people say you could be as good as Red Foster." She moved over so he could sit in the carriage with her. The driver moved to the front of his horse so that he could keep an eye on them. He adjusted the bridle and the chest strap and combed his horse's mane and foretop with his fingers. "I want you to meet my folks, I know if they get to know you they would like you."

"I met them both at the cookout."

"Yes, but they didn't get to talk with you, there were so many people there. I want it to be just the four of us."

"I don't know Leah. I am not...."

She interrupted him before he could state his case. "Johnny, please just do this for me. I want them to get to know you, to see what a great guy you are so that I don't have to sneak around." She put her hand over his and looked up with her big blue eyes.

Johnny had not told her about the man on the train. He was sure it was her parents that had paid him. They must know by now that he was unsuccessful. Would they send another, or more than one? Red had warned him to be on the lookout, not to walk down any dark alleys or even go for a walk alone after dark.

"Have you said anything to your parents about this?"

"No. I don't want to give them a chance to say they don't want to meet you."

"So, you just plan to spring me on them?"

"Johnny, once you agree to meet them, I will figure out the details. I just know that once they get to visit with you, they will see what a really nice guy you are."

He was thinking that it couldn't do any harm. They had already sent a man to rough him up. They couldn't think any less of him than they already do.

"Okay, I will do it just for you, but I don't think it will change their minds about me. The guy that is good enough for their daughter has to be more than a baseball player."

"Good. It will all be fine. Just you wait and see. Clarence, will you please drive us to Red's." Clarence patted his horse and went to the driver's platform where he took up the reins and turned out into the street.

Leah was excited about Johnny meeting her parents. This meeting would solve all her problems. She wanted to do it sometime this week, the sooner the better. She would let him know the details when she figured it all out. She was talking so fast it was difficult for him to follow everything. Johnny hoped for her sake that it worked out but he didn't have much faith that it would. He wanted to say something to help the situation but he didn't have a clue what it would be.

"All you have to do Johnny is just be yourself." They had pulled up in front of his place. People were coming and going it was a busy time of the day.

"Hey, it's Johnny Farmer. Great game Johnny. Look its Johnny Farmer." A fan who had been at the game drinking beer all afternoon was going to Red's to continue his celebration.

"See all the competition I have Johnny. Be humble, and don't let this fame change you. I like you just the way you are." She gave him a peck on the cheek and his hand went to his cheek so fast he almost dropped the sack he was carrying with his bat and glove in it.

CHAPTER THIRTY-TWO

They were at the big round table in the Winton House when the paper boy delivered the Chicago Tribune.

"Look at that headline." James handed Denise the paper.

"EXPLOSION AT THE DIXIE KILLS OWNERS"

The story went on to say that Charles and Layla Wilcox and at least two others had been killed by an explosion late last night at the Dixie Distillery on South Englewood. The accident occurred just after midnight and firemen were still going through the wreckage.

"Well, I guess that closes one of our cases." Paul Wheeler took the stack of papers they had on the Wilcox's and put them in a folder. He was holding the paper where Denise had quoted McDonald.

"You have done all that you need to do. You have given Chicago all the information it needs. Chicago wants to thank you for bringing this to their attention and I feel confident that Chicago will deal out justice."

"You think maybe this wasn't an accident?" James took the paper from Wheeler and handed it to Denise.

Again, this was not what she had envisioned. She had seen a courtroom, with a prosecutor listing their crimes, she had heard a jury saying they were guilty and a judge giving them a sentence. She wanted to see their faces, to let them know she had helped with their down fall. If this was justice, maybe it was revenge she had been looking for. Had she been fooling herself all these years?

"I just feel empty. The man that killed my father is dead and now the one's that ordered the assassination are dead." Denise was in a daze, she could not believe it was over. She had been driven by her need and desire to learn the truth about her father's death and to bring them to justice. But was it really justice she wanted or revenge?

"Are you okay?" James could see that Denise was perplexed, puzzled by all this.

"I need to go to the church. I need to pray and think."

"Would you like some company?"

"No thanks. I just need some time." She slowly got to her feet, handed James back the paper and made her way to the door.

"James, go down to your work place and see what you can learn. Try to find out why they were both down there at mid-night." Wheeler was still going through the pages on the Wilcox as he put them in the folder. They had a whole bunch of smoke but no real fire.

"Forgive me Father, for I have sinned." Denise was in the confessional at the Cathedral on State Street.

"The peace of God is about to put everything in place for you my child." The voice of the priest was comforting.

Denise continued to acknowledge her sins with true sorrow. She went into detail about her sinful pride and revengeful nature. The priest listened with extreme interest. This was not his normal confession of sins from drinking, gambling, or adultery.

After saying her penitence Denise felt much better. She walked out of the church to a beautiful boulevard lined with oak trees, she had not noticed them on her way in. She had a much better view of her world and her life. She felt strong that she could serve her Lord. Her faith was strong her vision was clear.

She was a much different person walking back to the Winton House. This had been an obsession with her and now it was coming to an end. She had lived her life with just this one goal in mind. Now she was free to branch out and take flight. She hurried up the steps to the Winton House.

"Where is James?"

"He went down to his work to see what he could learn about the accident."

James learned that the Wilcox's were summoned to the distillery because of the formation of a gas cloud in one of their warehouses. They had been to the theater, had stopped at the Country Club for a nightcap and was just leaving to go home when they got the message.

One of their employee's said he saw them walk into the storage area and very soon after they had entered the explosion sent oak barrels of whiskey through the roof. Burning whiskey flowed in all directions from the building.

A number of assumptions have been made but it has not been established what was the ignition source of the flammable gas cloud. The firemen were still going through the charred remains of the building. The building burned to the ground before the firemen could get to the scene. They were able to save several other buildings in the area that caught fire. They called it an accidental industrial accident. Was it, or was it Chicago dealing out justice. James was remembering what McDonald had told Denise.

"I suggest that you go back to your St. Louis convent, your work here is done. Get a Chicago paper to read each morning after your morning prayers. Let nature take its course."

"You have done all that you need to do. You have given Chicago all the information it needs. Chicago wants to thank you for bringing this to their attention and I feel confident that Chicago will deal out justice."

James wondered if things would change. Was this the end of their journey together? Would Denise be leaving to go back to the mission? Could this situation in Denver be just what they needed? So many questions, he hoped the answers would be to his liking. He was not ready to leave Denise and go back to Eagle Valley. She was his companion, the friend to whom he could confide and from whom he could obtain counsel.

CHAPTER THIRTY-THREE

Johnny stood off to the side of the Chicago City Cemetery almost out of sight. He did not want his being there to cause a disturbance. It was the interment of Leah's parents. He felt sure that she was going through stages of anger, sadness and heartache.

He was glad that he had not said anything to her about the man on the train. He did not want anything to change the loving memory she had of her parents. She had been so excited about getting him to meet with them. He hoped that her last memory with her mother was not their disagreement over him.

His thoughts drifted back to his parent's funeral. He was just a boy and did not understand why they were taken from him. His grandparents took him to live with them on their small farm just outside Randalia. Like most of the farms they had eight to ten milk cows, six to eight sows to raise, little pigs and chickens for fresh eggs. They didn't have much money but they always had good food and plenty of it.

Each October they would butcher a hog and a steer. Hang them in the ice house and have fresh pork and beef all winter. He went to Randalia to school. It was located in northeast Iowa, in the center of Fayette County. By the time he graduated from high school he knew everyone in town and all the farmers for miles around. He had also tasted soap from his Grams when he repeated a word he had heard at school.

He learned to swim in the Volga River and best of all he got to play baseball. When the high school had a home baseball game the whole town was there to watch and cheer. It was important to everyone in the community they play good, hard baseball. If one of the players did not run out a pop fly they heard about it everywhere they went. Winning was important but playing the game with pride and hustle was even more important. They forgave and forgot an error but they had an elephant's memory when it came to lack of hustle.

Nothing bad happens without some good coming from it. Johnny felt that was so true in his case. He had lost his parents but he gained Randalia. He hoped that Leah too would experience some good from this tragedy.

Johnny wished that he could help her, console her but for now all he could do was say a prayer for her and her parents. Johnny did not go to church much nor did he read the bible regularly. But he did not understand how anyone could grow up on a farm in Iowa and not believe in God. There were so many little miracles around the farm and everything fit together so perfect, there is no way it could have been an accident.

His Grams had taught him never to pray for a baseball victory or a good grade on a test. He was to pray for strength, courage and to always do his best. If he heard her say it once, he heard her say it a hundred times: "Johnny, if it worth doing, it is worth doing well. You always give it your best effort." She also taught him to thank the Lord for his food before each meal and to say his prayers before going to sleep each night.

As a small boy when he would say, "I wish." His Gramps would say, "Do not wish to be anything but what you are and be the best you that you can be."

Funerals always made him stop and realize how quickly life could be taken away. He would have to write his grandparents, he knew how much they looked forward to his letters. He watched as they lowered the caskets into the ground. He could see Leah stand and take a handful or dirt and put it in each of the graves. He was glad the team was leaving on a road trip right after today's game. It would give Leah some time to grieve before he saw her. He did not know what he should do or say to console and to comfort her.

He had to get to the ball park. He had already missed batting practice. Red had given him permission to be late but asked him to be at the game if at all possible. Slowly he turned, so many thoughts racing through his mind. He would be glad to get on the field he never had any trouble forgetting all other things and putting his mind totally on the game. It was as if he had a switch like on a railroad track that made the train go from one track to another. Once on the field his mind and concentration was completely on the game.

The team knew why Johnny was late so no one said anything to him about it. Had they not known or had it been because he overslept he would have got a steady bombardment of razing. A couple of the guys were great at playing pranks. As a rookie he was often the victim but he remembered when he had been teased his first days at school in Randalia. "Remember Johnny, boys never throw stones at trees without apples." Gramma Otto had gone on to explain what that meant. This had helped him with his self-esteem and he had few problems in school.

He had always let his play on the field do his talking and it had served him well. Communicating with Leah was never easy for him but at a time like this it was next to impossible. He wished everything could be as simple and easy for him to understand as baseball.

CHAPTER THIRTY-FOUR

"We don't need you to be working at the Dixie any longer. You can go in tomorrow and see if you can find out anything new and give them your notice. We will have to make a new game plan." Wheeler took his coffee and went to his office. Denise, James, Anderson, and Wolfgram were at the round table having their morning coffee.

James thought Denise was changed. She seemed more relaxed, like a weight had been lifted off her shoulders. He had never known her when she wasn't on her vigorous campaign to find out about her father's murder. She was suddenly seeing a world she had not seen since she was fifteen years old in St. Louis and it looked good on her.

"What great thing can we do today to make this a better world?" Denise got up to get the coffee pot and refill their cups. "You can finish that Washington report so I can get it printed and in the mail." Wolfgram held his cup out to her.

"You sure know how to bring a girl back to the here and now. I was hoping that some little elf had already done that. That's what we need around here a mischievous fairy. Know where we can order one of them?"

"I am learning that you can be mischievous enough without a little elf to help you out." Wheeler had come out of his office to get more coffee. "I am going over the Fire Marshall's report on the explosion at the Dixie Distillery to see if we need to investigate this Chicago justice that appears to have been dealt."

"You think this could have been a vigilante group dealing out Chicago justice instead of an accident?" James had thought this from the first time he saw the headline in the Tribune.

"I don't know but the Fire Marshall is calling it an accident. I have seen nothing in his report so far that would indicate any different. We will see if any of our men out in the field hear anything, in the mean time we have other fish to fry. Denise get yourself all dolled up and go to that Chicago Woman's Club luncheon, see if you can hear any gossip. James, I guess you could go now, turn in your resignation and see what you can learn. I got Mose going to Haymarket, so you will have to take a cab to the luncheon Denise, which could be better anyway."

Denise dressed in her finest and walked up to the hotel, in the back door and out the front to a waiting cab. The luncheon was at the Palmer House and Mrs. Goldsmith had a shrine for Layla Wilcox in the lobby. An oil portrait of her with candles and decorated with flowers. The program was a tribute to Mrs. Wilcox and all that she had done for the club. Denise did not speak to anyone, until they were seated to eat. She had dressed so as not to stand out. She was not wearing anything elaborate or anything on the down side so that she would be noticed. She listened to all the compliments paid to the deceased with interest. Mrs. Wilcox had not been one to do all the good that she could and not make a fuss about it. In fact it seemed that she made as much fuss about it as possible. People were coming up with all sorts of little things that she had done or that she had told them she had done.

Denise wanted to scream that this woman was evil, that she had paid someone to kill her father. That she was not who they all seemed to think she was. But she bite her tongue and said nothing. It would serve no purpose, she had to think of the big picture. It was not important what these women thought of Mrs. Layla Wilcox. Denise knew the truth and that was the important thing.

She was glad that she had not said anything negative as one of the first things Mrs. Goldsmith did was introduce Leah Wilcox. The young girl thanked them all for coming and for the tribute to her mother.

"I have received some rather large memorial gifts and I feel that my mother would want these to go to your club for you to use as you see fit. I will use some of the money to improve the Belmont Harbor and to take a group of orphans to a Chicago White Stockings game. I think she would approve of both of these. Thank you again for all the kind words." Leah took her seat to a standing ovation.

James learned that the distillery and the barrel making plant were being run by the executor of the Wilcox estate, the Chicago State Bank. There were young junior executives running around everywhere. The rumors were as many as the junior executives. The bank held a mortgage and would sell the property's to cover the amount still owed. James turned in his notice and was told that he could come on pay day and pick up the salary that was due. The bank was going to continue to run the business and cover the pay roll.

CHAPTER THIRTY-FIVE

Johnny was having a bad day. The ump would not call any strikes on the edges of the plate and the Cincinnati batters where not swinging unless the ball was down the middle of the plate. Johnny was getting hit hard and the White Stockings were getting beat. Johnny had not experienced this very much in the past, he was upset.

"That's the way it is sometimes on the road. Just do the best you can and don't worry about it. Keep changing speeds, I would rather they hit it than you walk them." Red had seen this happen before, it was tough to win on the road if the home team didn't go up to the plate hacking.

Johnny did his best but he gave up a season high of eight runs and the White Stockings suffered their second straight loss. It was nearing the end of the season and the White Stockings had a five game lead in the standings. They had two more games on this road trip and then a three game home series to end the season. All they had to do was win one more game to chinch the pennant.

Winning the pennant would mean a bonus to all the players and make them the toast of the town. Red had asked Johnny to work for him but Johnny had told him that he had to go visit his grandparents. They too were counting the games until the end of the season.

That night, Johnny didn't sleep well. He made several attempts to write a letter to Leah but couldn't do that either. He did get a short note to his grandparents. He got to vent on the umpire and that made him feel a little better. He knew that his grandfather did not like for him to complain about the calls in a ball game but he felt in this case he would understand.

The White Stockings suffered another loss to Cincinnati Red Stockings before boarding the train home. They had a three game series with the Philadelphia Centennials to end their season. Johnny was scheduled to pitch the third game of the series, the last game of the season. As it turned out it was not a big deal as the White Stockings sweep the series winning the pennant by three games.

After they won the first game of the series, Chicago celebrated and many of the fans were too hung over to come to the second game. In fact winning the first game cost the owners serious money. The first game was packed, some fans stood and some were turned away. The last two games they played to a less than capacity crowd.

This would be their last game in Lake Front Park. They had already started building the new field on the West side it would be ready for the 1882 season.

He had dinner with Leah after the second game as he planned to catch the train for Iowa after their final game.

"I wish you would take Red up on his offer and stay in Chicago for the winter." They were eating at Red's. It was what Leah wanted to do. It was not fancy. They were having Red Hot's and some of Red's famous Ox Tail Soup.

"I made my grandparents a promise that I would go back to the farm right after the season was over. I am all they have and they have done so much for me. I have to do this for them." Johnny dipped some sweet bread in his soup and took a bite.

"I know. I know it is the right thing for you to do but I would so like to have you in Chicago. Would you at least promise to come visit at least once during the winter?" Following Johnny's lead, she dipped her bread in the soup and took a bite. It may not be the best table manners for Chicago's high society but she had to admit it tasted good.

"I will do my best. I don't see why I couldn't come visit at least once. It is rather easy catching the trains." The next two days went by in a flash and Johnny said his good-byes to Chicago.

Johnny took the Illinois Central to Independence, Iowa and then the Rock Island up to Randalia. Before boarding the train to Randalia he changed clothes. He put on the same clothes he was wearing when he boarded the town in Randalia several months earlier. He did not want the people to think that he was changed, that he was some city slicker.

The Rock Island was a freight train and had only a caboose where Johnny road with the conductor. The train stopped in every small town if the flag were out or if it had freight to drop off. It took almost as much time to go the twenty-five miles north to Randaila as it did from Chicago to Independence.

No one knew Johnny was coming so there was no one at the depot in Randalia. He would walk the mile to his grandparent's farm. He had discarded the cardboard suitcase and the flour sack. The saddle maker had made him a nice leather bag for his baseball gear and he had a large leather case for his clothes.

Somebody saw him get off the train and walk to his grandparents and the word spread like wild fire that Johnny was back. It only took them a couple days to plan a welcome home party at the WRC Hall. They had the town band there to play. Mable Mabon on piano, Art Spatcher on drums and Fred Grant on fiddle. It was pot luck and the place was full of good people and good food.

The older folks liked to square dance. They knew the dances so well they would do the moves before the caller sang them out. Allemande left and couples circulate. They swung their partners to the music coming from the balcony, three squares of eight to a square.

When the band took a short break and then broke into Cotton-eyed Joe it was the young kids turn to show off their dancing talent. This traditional folk dance was fun for both those dancing and those just watching. It was difficult not to clap or stomp your feet to the beat of the music.

"O Cotton-eyed Joe, O Cotton-eyed Joe,

What did make you sarve me so?

O Joe, if it hadn't ben fur you,

I'd er married dat gal fur true."*

Johnny didn't dance, he was busy talking to people he had not seen all summer and telling them of his experiences playing baseball in Chicago. When it came time to eat he was asked to say Grace and be the first to fill his plate with all the delicious food.

Sunday morning was much the same way. You would have thought it was Easter or Christmas at the Methodist Church. The place was packed when they learned that Johnny would be there. They had to open the folding doors into the eating area for the over flow crowd.

Johnny and his grandparents came to church in the grain wagon as they did not have a buggy. His grandparents were on the spring seat and Johnny stood behind. It was not far and it was such a nice fall day, the leaves had turned and the big maple trees were in their best fall colors.

*The origins of this song are unclear although it pre-dates our American Civil War.

Johnny had never seen his grandparents so proud. He had never heard them sing so loud or as well as they did today. The pastor also got into the occasion as he preached to this packed church.

He told the people to just ask. "Do you wish you had more faith? Ask! Do you wish to be a better Christian? Ask! Do you wish to be a better parent? Ask! Do you wish to a better son or daughter? Ask!" Each time he yelled "Ask" he banged his hand on the pulpit. Several that had drifted off to sleep were awaken by the sudden and violent noise that sounded like a rifle shot.

"You will find, as you look back upon your life, that the moments when you have really lived are the moments when you have done the Lord's work in a spirit of love."

CHAPTER THIRTY-SIX

The big coal burning locomotive chug-chugged across the Mississippi River into Iowa on its way to Denver. The shrill sound of the train's whistle drifted back to the Pullman coach where James and Denise were enjoying their first class accommodations. They were taking advantage of the perks traveling as agents of the Department of Treasury.

The thousand miles of track between Chicago and Denver would take days. Depending on how long and how many stops they made if it would be two or three days. They should have good weather to travel, it was too early for snow and too late for the hot humid weather of an Iowa summer.

Their Pullman had nice comfortable padded velvet seats that folded down into beds. Curtains that closed for privacy. The dining car was just ahead of them and they had the pleasure of the diverse menu. They did not have to worry about the cost of the meal as Uncle Sam was picking up their tab.

Wheeler had encouraged them to take this business vacation. They were going to Denver for both business and pleasure. They would talk to the Denver people about opening an office and they would have time to visit. There were already Federal Marshall's in Colorado but the Department of Treasury did not have an office.

The motion of the train ground to a stop and James opened his eyes and listened. They were taking on water and coal. Some passengers were departing and others were boarding the train to travel west. Mail was being picked up and dropped off. It was almost daybreak so James thought he would get up and get a jump on the men's washroom before it got busy.

James was in the dining car eating hot cakes, sausage and enjoying his coffee when Denise found him. As she took a seat across from him the waiter handed her a menu.

"I will have an egg over easy some toast and coffee please." The waiter took the cup that was in front of her, turned it over and filled it with hot coffee. He took the menu and went to the kitchen at the end of the car.

"Did you sleep well?" Denise blew on her coffee before taking a sip.

"Yes, I slept very well until this morning when I heard the train whistle. How about you, did you sleep well?"

"Yes, the motion of the train and the clicking of the wheels seemed to help me. I did tend to wake up every time we made a stop but had no problem going back to sleep again once we were moving. For years I have been seeing through eyes looking for a clue, hearing with ears listening for a sound to help solve a mystery and thinking with a brain that was obsessed with finding answers to my father's murder. Now I can see, hear and think of things in a different way. I can enjoy them for just what they are."

"I must say that I have noticed a difference and I like the change. I liked the old Denise but I like the new Denise even more." James took his napkin off his lap and placed it on the table beside his clean plate.

"It appears that James also likes to travel first class, you seem to have adopted to the change rather well."

"Yes it is not difficult going from second class to first class. I am guessing that once accustomed to first class going back to second class would be more difficult."

The waiter came with Denise's breakfast and more hot coffee. While they were at breakfast, the porter in the Pullman was changing their beds back into comfortable seats. The service traveling first class was exceptional.

The trip across Iowa was fast and smooth, the train stopped in Iowa City, Des Moines and Council Bluffs where it crossed the Mighty Mo. into Omaha, Nebraska. Before 1873 when the bridge was built, passengers had to get off the train in Council Bluffs and ride coaches over a ferry to Omaha where they could board another train west. This made Omaha the poor Red Headed step sister to Kansas City when it came to rail travel.

The tracks out of Omaha followed the North Platte River to Sidney and west to Kimball. This being flat country like Iowa, the train made good time reaching speeds of forty miles per hour. In western Nebraska the tracks began to climb and once into Colorado the elevation gradually got higher and the train went slower.

They were just twenty miles east of Denver coming into Strasburg when the train made an abrupt stop. Later they learned that a large bon-fire had been built on the tracks. They also learned that a large shipment of currency was on board to buy gold. The U.S. paper money was backed with gold and the Department of Treasury would ship bank notes to buy gold that was shipped back to Fort Knox.

The robbers did not take any chances going from car to car. They broke into the mail car, found the sack of National Gold Bank notes for the Colorado Gold and Silver Exchange and were gone in just a matter of minutes.

It took the train crew longer to remove the bon-fire from the tracks than it did for the robbers to steal the money. The bills were all in the denomination of one hundred dollars. The bills were commonly referred to as "Benjamins" or "C" notes. They had a picture of Benjamin Franklin on the obverse and an image of Independence Hall on the back.

It took only minutes for the news to spread through the train of the robbery. James and Denise knew this was a big hit on the Department of Treasury and that Washington would want some action taken. It appeared they had their first big case and they were not even in Denver.

The robbery was well planned and well executed. None of the passengers had an opportunity to maybe recognize any of the gang. Colorado was a real honey hole of convenient riches to rob. The people did not look upon a train robbery where they did not shoot up the train or take anything from the passengers near as serious as a claim jumper.

Colorado comes from a Spanish word meaning red or ruddy. The color of much of the states terrain. The state was also being noted for its dry climate and was considered favorable for curing respiratory diseases, tuberculosis in particular. Many on the train were coming from the East coast looking for a cure.

The Union Station in Denver was packed with people, many like Denise and James looking for a cab to take them to a hotel. After a short wait they got one and were on their way to the Windsor. There were several telegrams waiting for them at the desk. One from Washington and two from Wheeler.

They were to find some office space, set up an office and get to work on the train robbery. They had been sent a list of the serial numbers on the bills that were stolen. They had to get these numbers to the banks in the area so that they could report to them any bills that might be in circulation. Maybe more important was to get the numbers to places like the Red Dog Saloon and General Stores. A hundred dollars was a lot of money and anyone that had a hundred dollar bill was a suspect.

The Rocky Mountain News carried the story of the train robbery and gave credit to the Burrows Gang. The write up in the paper made it sound like the Burrows Gang were the good guys.

While James was going to all the big saloons and general stores, Denise found a nice office building. It was on Larimer Street in the Union Station neighborhood of Denver. It also had living quarters up stairs with two nice bedrooms, a kitchen and living room. It was all furnished so all they had to do was move in.

Washington had transferred money for them to the Denver National Bank, so all they had to do was sign banks notes or go to the bank and draw out cash.

It did not take them long to learn that Denver was much like Chicago. Here too, underworld bosses worked side by side with city officials and the police. Eddie Chase, Denver's Mike McDonald, regularly entertained Denver's most influential leaders. Gambling flourished and bunco artists exploited every opportunity they had to separate miners from their hard-earned diggings.

Denver was experiencing corruption as well as progress. They had their work cut out for them, they could see that it would be a marathon and not a sprint.

CHAPTER THIRTY-SEVEN

James was riding a horse he rented at the livery stable, it was easier to rent when he needed one as it was rare that his work took him out of Denver.

He could smell the Ponderosa Pine and the Spruce as he rode into the valley. On both sides were towering walls of rock and in front of him was the magnificent valley. He saw horses and cattle grazing on the rich green grass all of them wearing the eagle brand. He could hear the trout stream as it ran over the rocks next to the canyon wall.

James never knew that coming back to the valley could be so much fun. The kids were all over him with as almost as many questions as Judith. The only one that wasn't real sure was Squirt. She had been too young to remember her Uncle James. But she guessed that if Chet and Sarah thought he was a good guy she would take a chance and it wasn't long before she crawled up on his lap.

Caroline Kaye was already walking and saying, "No". She was little but she knew what she wanted and what she didn't want. James had to smile as he could see Kemp was going to have his hands full with this little gal. Luta was the only one that she seemed to mind without even thinking. If he asked her to do something she did it immediately.

The sun was starting to sink behind the mountains by the time he got to his folks cabin. His mother hugged him so hard and long and he thought he could see a tear in the eye of his father. They too had question after question for him.

"In the morning I would like to go to the stream and catch a mess of trout. I have not been fishing or had any good trout since I rode out of here." They were all talked out, it was bed time and his old room was just as he remembered it.

The most difficult question for James was how was his relationship with Denise? Even he did not know the answer to that question. Telling them that they got along fine, were good friends, and enjoyed working together. That she wanted to meet them but thought she should go first and visit the mission did not seem to appease them.

He woke up to the smell of pork belly and coffee. Some things don't ever seem to change. But he knew it would never be the way it was. Even now he was thinking about things he should be doing in Denver.

After breakfast his mother walked out with him. Looking up she saw a pair of eagles on the old Ponderosa Pine high upon the south rim of the canyon. "James, the eagles are back. This is the first time I have seen them since you left."

"Most likely they are just stopping on their way south for the winter. Most of their fishing holes will be froze over in another month. Speaking of fishing, are the poles still hanging in the shed?"

"Yes, your father tied some new flies and they are in the vest hanging with the poles."

James slipped the vest on and took a pole to the spring fed stream behind the cabin. It did not take him long to catch enough fish for the three of them. He looked at the clear, clean water and wished the people of the city could enjoy this. Many of them had never even seen anything like this. Too many were born, raised, and died in the city without ever experiencing this.

The trout were as good as he remembered. His mother also had fresh baked bread, potatoes and a huckleberry pie. This too was something many of the people in the city had never experienced.

"Will you be able to go to church with us in the morning?" His father knew the trip to Denver was long and he knew James had to get back for work on Monday morning.

"Yes, I would like to attend church and eat with you before I leave for Denver." He reached for another piece of pie that was still warm from the oven.

Most churches had one side for the men and the other for the women and there was no mixed seating. In fact many had a different door for the women and men to go into the church. There was no soft glances nor tender hand clasps. Penny and Judith had talked about this and they wanted to start right out in family units. They didn't know if Jokob would object but Judith said she would handle him. She knew how much he liked a good smoke and that too was frowned on. The women did cover their heads when in church. It could be a veil or an ornate bonnet but they did not enter church uncovered.

Wade and his family had one pew, Kemp and his family another and Sweeny and his family the third. James's mother was seated at the organ and Jokob had a chair up near the pulpit. This made James the odd man out. He had thought about it, he was a Schroeder so maybe he should sit with Kemp and his family.

As he walked into the church the problem seemed to be solved. Squirt and little Caroline were on the fourth pew with a space for him in between them. They both looked up and patted the seat for their Uncle James.

"Lord God, our heavenly father, bless this thy house that it may endure forever. We thank thee Lord for your gifts which we receive from your bountiful goodness. Thank you for watching over us and for bringing James home if only for a visit. We ask these things in the name of our savior and your son, Jesus. Amen."

His mother played the doxology. "Jesus Loves Me" followed and then "Holy Holy Holy". She had no music, she had to play from memory. They had no song books but they had been singing these songs all their lives so they knew the words.

Jokob's message was of thanks and praise. Thanking Lord for all they enjoyed in the valley and praising him for all the he gave them. He asked the Lord to help them set their minds on things above, not on earthly things. "Lord God of love, fill us with Your love, and help us put it into action. Amen"

On the long ride back to Denver James had hours to think about his situation and his visit back to Eagle Valley. He was surprised at how good he felt when Squirt or Caroline would grab his finger or jump into his lap.

Life was so simple, so serene in the valley, he wished that he could somehow bottle it and give it to the people of Chicago. He felt so lucky that he could go there and experience it whenever he wanted to.

CHAPTER THIRTY-EIGHT

"Come in, Denise. It is good to see you." Father Heilman was tall with broad shoulders, blond hair and spoke with a slight German accent.

Denise thought the office looked the same, the desk was cluttered with papers and books. It was in need of a good dusting and his chair still had the same squeak when he stood up.

Denise told Father Heilman all that had happened. Well, most of what had happened and she learned from him that Sister Mary had gone back to St. Louis.

"Many of the children are still here. Some have been placed and of course some new one's have taken their place." They were walking out into the court yard. As Denise looked up, she saw an eagle soaring on the thermal currents high overhead.

The eagle is the winged symbol of many people because it is seen as the strongest and bravest of all birds. The Indians wore the feathers of the eagle on their heads and on their horses. The eagle and its feathers were treated with great respect by both the Indian and the white man. Eagles are often considered to be a spiritual messenger between their Gods and Native Americans.

Denise could not help but remember the eagle she saw as she was leaving on her adventure. Wishing at the time that she could be so strong and free. Now she wondered if it were a spiritual messenger between her and her Lord. Did he approve of what she had done and what she was doing?

The mission school seemed the same but it was different. The difference being that she was not a part of it. She had to come and pay her respects but she was learning that she could not turn back the clock. Things could never be as they were.

Father Heilman sensed Denise was having a struggle. He had an understanding as this was not the first time he had witnessed these circumstances. There were no magic words that he could say.

"I wish I could spend more time with the children. I find myself more and more chained to my desk. I am still doing the Lord's work but not as I would prefer to do it." He held the door for her to enter the hall leading to the classrooms.

Suddenly, Denise had seen and heard enough. She finished the tour and thanked Father Heilman but the question she had, was answered.

Walking down Mountain Street toward the train station the sweet smell of hops was in the air. Adolph Coors had built a brewery and took advantage of the spring water. Golden City was situated between Lookout Mountain and the two Table Mountains in a sheltered valley fed by Clear Creek which flows from the west through town. Just twelve miles west of Denver, Golden City had been the capital of the Colorado Territory.

Colorado became the 38th state of the Union in 1876, it took sixteen years, four Colorado votes and three different suggested state constitutions before it was finally approved.

Why did it take so long? First, there was a clash of egos of prominent Coloradans. Then there was the tightwad philosophy of the early settlers and last but not least, the bitter fight between President Andrew Johnson and the Republicans. Andrew Johnson was placed on the ticket with Lincoln as a "War Democrat". The Republican leadership thought he would strengthen the ticket. The Republican leadership never thought he would become President.

Colorado had not changed, there was still a clash of egos in Denver and Denise was thinking about this as she walked to her train. Frederick Walker Pitkin was the Governor of Colorado. A Republican with contacts in the mining industry. He had declared martial law during the mining strike in Leadville in 1880. Charles A. Arthur, a Republican was the President of the United States after the assassination of James Garfield.

Both of these men wanted to see law and order come to the United States. That was the reason she and James had been sent to Denver to open the office. Colorado was rich with resources and because of this it was also a breeding ground for corruption. Much like Chicago it was difficult to tell who was who as the criminal element worked hand in hand with the city and state officials.

Denise felt it was time for her to live neither in the past or in the future. She wanted to use her energies to satisfy her daily ambitions. She could not wait to see if James felt the same way. She felt that her life had not been her own. She had been on a mission and now it was over.

CHAPTER THIRTY-NINE

Johnny boarded the south bound train in Randalia and waved goodbye to his grandparents seated in the grain wagon. He was nervous, just as uneasy has he had been in May when he first went to Chicago. But this time it was for a different reason. This time he didn't have so much confidence in his ability. He believed in his heart that he was a good baseball player, that he was worthy of playing with the White Stockings. He didn't know if he was worthy of Leah, in his heart he felt she was a class above him.

She had been writing letter after letter asking him to come to Chicago to visit. She told him in her last letter that if he didn't come by Christmas she was coming to Randalia. That was enough to get him moving as he did not have a clue what he would do with her in Randalia or at his grandparent's farm.

It was just three days until Christmas so the nearer the train got to Chicago the more people that were aboard. By the time it pulled into Union Station it was packed.

The bank had sold the big house and purchased a nice brown stone house for Leah just north of Lincoln Park. It was a three bed room home that Leah shared with Hilda, her housekeeper maid, nanny, and friend. She had told Johnny that she wanted him to stay in the guest bedroom. He had the address in his pocket but felt he would be more comfortable at Red's if there was an empty room.

Johnny had never been in Chicago in the winter and the wind coming off Lake Michigan was ice cold. It was also mixed with driving snow that added to the miserable conditions. People were hailing cabs and almost fighting for them. He thought he would walk the few blocks to Red's when he spotted a cab driver holding up a sign with his name on it. He walked up to him and before he could say anything the man reached for his bag.

"Hello Johnny. How was your train ride?" He took the bag and placed it in the cab. Holding the door for Johnny to step inside, "Mother Nature is making things a little unpleasant but it is not far to a warm house and Miss Leah."

The next few days were a whirlwind to Johnny. Leah with her charm and energy made him relax and feel comfortable. With Hilda's help he got her an appropriate Christmas gift. Hilda helped wrap it and see that it was under the tree when Leah got up on Christmas morning.

Johnny had planned to leave a few days after Christmas but Leah talked him into staying for New Year's Eve as she had a surprise for him. Christmas and New Years in Chicago was just one new experience after another for Johnny. With Leah and Hilda's help and guiding he got along fine.

It was January second and he had his bag packed when he came down for breakfast. He sat his bag by the door and noticed two other large bags already there. He walked to the kitchen and found Leah dressed in traveling clothes. She was at the table with a cup of coffee and a smile from ear to ear.

"My surprise is a gift to me. I am going to find out what is so special about this Randalia. I am going with you and I do not want to discuss it." She poured him a cup of coffee and Hilda put a plate of bacon and eggs in front of him.

Later, Johnny picked up his bag and put it under his arm as he had seen drivers do and picked up Leah's bags. The weight of them almost made him sit them back down. "How long do you plan to stay, did you take all the clothes that you own?"

"Girls require a little more then you guys. As for how long I stay, long enough for me to learn why Randalia is such a wonderful place."

With Leah the train ride did not seem so long. It was the first time she had ever been west of Chicago and she had lots to see and many questions to have answered. Going over the Mississippi and into Iowa was exceptional for both of them.

At Independence they switched to the Rock Island freight train. Leah charmed the conductor riding with them in the caboose to the point that he fixed them hot coffee and shared some cookies his wife had made.

There was no one at the depot in Randalia except the depot agent. He said he would watch their bags for them an apologized for not having a rig that they could use. They had walked only a few hundred yards when Mr. Arthur, who lived east of Johnny's grandparents stopped to give them a lift. When he asked where their bags were, he turned the team and went back to get them.

When they got to the farm, Johnny's grandfather was on his way to the barn to milk the cows. He liked to milk at the same time each morning and afternoon. He thanked Mr. Arthur and helped Johnny to the house with the bags. When Leah found out where he was going and what he was going to do, she wanted to go too. Johnny said he would change clothes and be right out. They put Leah's things in his room, he would have to sleep upstairs where the only heat was the stove pipe and what came up the stair way.

When he got to the barn he found Leah with a milk pail between her legs on a three legged stool under their old roan cow. Rosie would give her milk easy but Leah was having a little trouble getting the hang of it. The cat was waiting for a drink and Johnny wished he had a tintype he could show Hilda.

Leah learned to love Randalia and Randalia returned her love. They didn't do anything special, just the normal life on the farm and going to town. They had to take milk to the creamery and eggs into the store. Leah was outside as much as she was in the house. Even the old rooster who didn't like anyone coming in his hen house didn't seem to mind Leah.

Rosie became her cow to milk and she got so that she could milk her while Johnny and his grandfather each milked three. The seven cows each gave a big pail of milk morning and night. So every three days they had to haul three big ten gallon milk cans to the creamery.

On Sunday they went to the service at the Methodist church and stayed for pot luck dinner. Leah had never seen so much good food served to so many so fast. Each family came with a big basket and their own table service. When everyone had eaten each lady would pick up her dishes and it was all cleaned up in just minutes. If whatever the lady brought was all gone she had a smile but if a dish was only half gone she wondered why nobody liked it and her husband would hear about it on the way home.

Johnny took Leah to the school where he proudly showed her the trophy case. The big three story brick school held grades first through twelve. Johnny had gone to school from grade three and many of his teachers were still teaching. They all wanted Johnny and Leah to stop in their classroom and tell the class about Chicago. What was to be a short tour of the school turned out to be an all-day affair.

One day in the store Leah got to meet Johnny's biggest fan and mentor, Fred Grant. Fred already knew everything about Leah as he had spoken with Johnny for hours about his summer in Chicago.

All too soon it was time for Leah to catch the train back to Chicago. "You can't let her make the trip to Chicago alone." Johnny's grandfather was not asking a question, he was letting Johnny know what he had to do. Johnny nodded his head in agreement.

"I guess this means I am going to have to go back to gathering the eggs and milking old Rosie."

"I will be back in a couple days Grams, I will just see Leah to her place and turn around and come back." Johnny didn't know it but Leah was standing right behind his chair.

"Don't make a promise you can't keep. I just may hogtie you and keep you in Chicago."

There was a group of people at the depot to see Leah off and to wish her a quick return. They had a basket of food for them to take on the train. She had made a good impression on Randalia.

Later as they were riding to the click and clang of the train Leah took her head off Johnny's shoulder and sat up. "It is not the place, it is the people. There is nothing special about Randalia but everything is special about the people of Randalia. To be on a first name bases with everyone is something I never dreamed possible. I can totally see why you wanted to spend your off season in Randalia. I can't wait to go back again." She returned her head to his shoulder, closed her eyes and drifted off to sleep.

Chapter Forty

"James, how do you feel about me?"

"Denise, is this one of those questions that no matter how I answer it I am in trouble?" James had been standing looking out the window into the street thinking about what he should do next.

"No" laughing, she added "I mean do you love me?"

"I don't know much about feelings but from the first time I saw you in the train station I wanted to be with you. I knew you were a Nun but for some reason I still had to be near you. If that is love, I guess I have always loved you."

"But you have never even made an attempt to kiss me."

"At first I didn't think it was appropriate and then I felt that you would let me know if you wanted me to." He turned from the window and walked to where she was seated at the desk.

"Well, either I am real bad at giving signs or you are bad at reading them. I have decided to start living for each day and in order to do that I have to find out where we stand." She stood up and moving around the desk she put her hands on his shoulders and looked up into his eyes.

There was a knock on the door and when James turned, one of the U.S. Marshall's working with them walked in. "The Nugget down on Market Street took in one of the bank notes from the train robbery. When I told him that it was stolen property and that I couldn't give him a good one in its place he got real unhappy. He said that would be the last time he would be working with us."

"So he told you to tell us that?" Denise reached for the bank note he held.

"Well Ma'am, he did use different words but that was the jest of it."

"James, we need to send Wheeler a gram. We can't expect people to work with us if it is going to cost them a hundred dollars every time they help us." She went to the desk and unlocked the drawer. She took out five twenty dollar bank notes and handed them to Marshall Clark.

"Go back to the Nugget and give him these and see if that helps him to remember what the guy looked like, who was with him and anything else that will help us."

Marshall Clark turned on his heel and went out the door. "That about wiped out our petty cash, so we need some help or advice from Wheeler."

"I'll go send a wire and then I will stop at the Nugget and see if Clark got things smoothed out. The last thing we need is for the word to get around that we seized the money and they are left holding the bag." James gabbed his hat and coat off the hook by the door and went out. Once out in the fresh mountain air he looked up and thanked the Lord for the knock on the door. It was not that he didn't want this conversation with Denise and what he hoped would follow, it was just that didn't seem like the proper time and place.

Many had removed the wheels and replaced them with runners as the streets were snow covered. In some places it was packed and almost like ice. A sleigh was coming up the street with a string of bells and many of the stores showed the signs of Christmas that was just days away.

As James passed Olson's Jewelry he paused to look in the window. He still had not gotten Denise a Christmas gift. He had seen her eye the long coat in the dry goods store one day and later went to check it out. It was made of all wool with large collars and lapels made of beaver and it was lined throughout with satin. It was priced at thirteen dollars and fifty cents which he thought was a little steep. He was still thinking about the coat when he found himself in the shop.

"What may I show you today?" The man was short, bald and spoke with a foreign accent. He had an eye shade and a funny thing attached to his glasses.

"I was looking for a Christmas gift for my girlfriend." James was looking down into a case that contained rings, lockets, stick pins and hat pins.

"Are you engaged to be married?"

"Well, not at the present, but I was thinking of asking." James's voice got weak toward the end as if he was not real sure what he was saying.

"We have some of the newest in engagement rings. This one is very nice, it has two very fine rose diamonds and two large fire opals, it is priced at eight dollars and these are all genuine rose cut diamonds in solid 14 karat gold through and through. This ring has eight rose diamonds in a circle, it is nine dollars and ninety-five cents. We also have this new style solitaire diamond in a fancy mounting, the rose diamond is a little larger and it is eight dollars and fifty cents. All these rings come with a velvet lined gift box. If you would really like to impress your lady we have this large one karat table cut diamond with six rose diamonds around it for one hundred and twenty dollars." He did not hand this one to James but just pointed to it in the case.

James did not know. It would be cheaper to buy Denise a ring than to get the coat. This surprised him. This would also be a way for him to show her how he felt and what his intentions were.

"Do you see anything that you think she would like?" The accent was north European, Swedish he guessed. "We also have some cheaper rings, mother of pearl and royal blue glass. These run around four or five dollars depending on the setting."

"I like this solitaire diamond, but I do not know what size to get." James picked up the box and was holding it in the sunlight coming through the front window.

"Try it on your little finger." James put it on his little finger and it came up to the first knuckle. "Does that look to be about the size of

173

her ring finger? You could always give it to her and after Christmas if it does not fit we will size it for you at no charge. That is a very nice ring, it is simple yet elegant and it tends to show good taste."

"I will take this ring, if it doesn't fit we will be back after Christmas." He was holding the ring in his left hand between his thumb and forefinger to examine it more closely when the door burst open.

Two men with guns drawn and kerchiefs over the faces rushed into the shop. James made the ring seem to disappear as he had seen his father do many times. He held his hands up, palms out.

They each had a sugar sack and they threw these onto the counter. "Fill them with everything in the cases and the cash drawer."

The jeweler took one of the sacks and began putting things from the case into it. He was bent down behind the counter, all they could see was his one hand taking things from the case. When he came to the hidden revolver his hand closed on the butt and he thumbed back the hammer. This was an unmistakable sound to all in the room.

The robber with his weapon on James, turned and fired. His slug hit the jeweler in the forehead slamming him back into the wall. With both men's attention on the jeweler, James drew his Modele revolver from his shoulder holster and shot the robber. The other man fired at James hitting him and making him spin along the counter. He fired at James again and raced for the door.

In just minutes the place was full of law officers and citizens. "This guy is still alive, somebody get him to the sawbones." The sheriff was pulling the mask off the dead robber as Marshall Clark entered. "That is Jake Burrows, I got a wanted poster on him." The sheriff was going through his pockets as he talked. "Get a posse together." He ordered one of his deputies standing by the door.

Marshall Clark hurried to tell Denise the news before he rode with the posse. "James has been shot. He is at the doctor's office. I have to ride with the posse. The sheriff found several hundred dollar "C" notes from the train robbery on the dead robber so we may solve two crimes with one arrest."

Denise did not hear anything after "He is at the doctor's office." She was grabbing her coat and hurrying out the door. It was only a few blocks to the doctor's office but she was out of breath when she got there.

"I got his wounds plugged and the bleeding stopped. He got hit once in the side of his neck. The bullet just missed both the breast bone and the collar bone. He was also shot in the back and it came out just above his right hip. It didn't hit any bone or vital organs so he was lucky. He lost enough blood to kill some men. He is out from the shock and the loss of blood but if he doesn't get infection he has a chance to live." He was busy cleaning up as he talked.

"I wonder what he was doing in the shop?" She said it out loud but it was more to herself than to the doctor.

"I don't know but he had this clenched in his left hand." He held up the solitaire diamond ring.

"Oh My!" Denise took it from the doctor and slipped it on her finger. She looked at the ring on her finger and then at James. "James, you are not going to die on me now. You hear me!" She brushed back the hair from his forehead and felt to see if he was running a fever. "James, you have to fight! James I need you to live!

CHAPTER FORTY-ONE

Johnny was back from escorting Leah home. He was taking the milk to the creamery and picking up some things at the store. He was greeted with much the same wherever he went or whoever he talked to: "Did Leah get home okay?" "That Leah is a keeper." "We sure did enjoy Leah." "You better latch on to Leah, we sure did like her." "What did Leah think of Randalia, did she like us as much as we liked her?"

His Gram was at the stove when he walked in and put the things from town on the table. "Any news from Town?"

"Just that Leah was the only thing anyone could talk about."

With a smile and chuckle she replied, "Did somebody have his ego bruised?"

"No, but it would have been nice if they would of at least said hello before they asked about Leah." He took a chair at the table and reached for a cookie from the big bear jar that always seemed to have fresh cookies in it.

"Well, she did impress me. She would sit and clean the chicken poop off the eggs or go out to the barn and enjoy milking old Rosie. I never saw her wrinkle up her nose at anything. She said 'thank you' and 'please' and was always pretty as a picture." She turned from the stove and took a seat across from Johnny at the table.

"I know. She impressed me too. I did not know how she would fit in or if she would even be able to stand it here. She not only enjoyed it she said she couldn't wait to come back again."

"Sounds to me like that young lady has her eyes set on you. How do you feel about her?" She took off her glasses and cleaned them with her apron.

"I like her. She can be pushy but she is also considerate. She is strong, she did not collapse with the death of her parents, not once did she ask why God let it happen. She grieved and then seemed to move on and do what she had to do. I am sure there are times when she is depressed but she doesn't use it as a crutch."

"Sounds to me that you should listen to those people you talked to in town. Besides that, your Gramps likes her and he has excellent taste in women." She got up and went back to the stove, it would soon be lunch time.

Johnny started throwing the baseball in the hay loft. He made a wood square the size of the strike zone and the hay piled against the wall cushioned the ball so that it did not splitter the end of the barn. He also did some running and exercises along with his daily farm chores. He had a letter from Red and he was to be in Chicago at least two weeks before the team went south for their spring games.

Johnny liked the feeling of just stepping out onto the baseball field as a player, whether it was practice or a game, it had such meaning to it. Maybe it was because baseball teams were like a family. There was something very special about baseball for Johnny. Just like he never wanted to let his grandparents down, he didn't want to let his teammates down.

This would be the first time he would not be here to help get the ground ready and plant the crops. He had ordered from the catalogue new Montana Concord harness and bridles with blinds and brass trim. They came with cotton cord mesh fly nets. His gramps was forever repairing the old harness that tended to break at the worst times. He also ordered a farmers canopy top surrey with upholstered cushions and backs for them to drive to church on Sunday. For his grandmother he ordered the Genuine improved Scott's washing machine. It had the pinwheel agitator and a wringer attached. The catalogue said the machine works easier than any other machine on the market. She used the wash board now and had to wring the clothes out by hand. He had stopped at the depot but they had not come in yet. Johnny knew these were things they would not buy for themselves, they would make do with what they had. Johnny had his bonus money for the team winning the pennant and he thought this was the best way he could spend it. The new harness cost fifteen dollars and the surrey was forty-three. The washing machine was ten dollars. The shipping was twelve dollars so he still had twenty bonus dollars to spend on himself.

He had also talked to the neighbors about asking to trade help planting and making hay. He knew his grandfather would never ask but he also knew he would never turn down a chance to help a neighbor. By helping the neighbor he would get help in return. It was almost impossible to farm without some help.

He was cleaning out the lean-to on the north side of the house to make room for the new washing machine. It was used for storage of things they didn't use but thought were too good to throw away. He found the rocking horse he had rode for miles, shooting outlaws and rounding up wild horses. A pair of barrel shaft ski's he had made that never did glide over the snow as he envisaged they would. A couple of bamboo fishing poles with line and cork bobbers still on them. He was sitting with a box of his school papers that his grandmother had saved when she opened the door.

"Johnny, pray tell what are you doing? Didn't you hear me call you to lunch? Your grandfather is waiting and the soup is getting cold." She stood holding the door with one hand and motioning with the other for him to get moving.

"Sorry, I thought I would straighten up the lean-to a little. Found some things I had forgotten about." He got to his feet and hurried to get washed up for lunch.

"Johnny said that everyone in town had good things to say about Leah."

"What's not to like? That gal has a good head on her shoulders and it's a pretty head to boot." He pointed to the crackers, his way of asking for them to be passed.

"I told Johnny you had good taste in women." She had to chuckle as she passed the crackers.

"She does remind me some of you at that age, remember when we went to that barn raising down by Twin Bridges?"

"Yes, do I ever! Think that barn raising produced Johnny's mother."

Johnny almost chocked on his soup. He had heard more that he wanted to hear. He had never heard them reminiscing like this. They sounded so pleased with their memories. He wondered if he and Leah would make moments worth remembering.

CHAPTER FORTY-TWO

James seemed to be doing well. He came to and Denise spoon fed him some broth. He went back to sleep and seemed to be resting comfortably. Denise was at his bedside when she noticed the fever coming on. It was not long and James was burning up with fever. The wound on his neck looked to be fine but the one above his hip was red and swollen.

Marshall Clark had come back with the posse and the two remaining members of the Burrows gang so Denise asked him to ride to the valley and let them know about James.

The doctor cleaned and redressed the wound and Denise kept cold cloths on his forehead but the fever got worse and James was delirious.

James's mother and father arrived late that night. His mother took one look at the infected wound and sent Jokob to the General Store. She applied raw honey to the wound and then covered it with raw bacon and bond it tightly.

The women took turns keeping cold cloths on James forehead and spoon feeding him beef broth. Getting any of the broth in his mouth was difficult as he was in a state of delirium. He would rant and thrash violently. He tossed about in the bed, his body fighting the infection.

"How is he, any better?" Jokob was at the kitchen table reading his bible.

"No, if anything, he is worse. It is in the Lord's hands." Mrs. Schroeder felt that she and Denise had done their best. She felt that James was fighting and doing his best. They would wait the result in peace.

EPILOGUE

Denise nursed James back to health and they spent their lives helping to bring law and order to Colorado. They raised a son and daughter that liked nothing better than to go visit their grandparents in Eagle Valley.

Johnny and Leah were married in The Randalia Methodist Church and had their wedding dance in the WRC Hall. The people of Randalia thought half of Chicago had invaded them but by midnight you couldn't tell the city slickers from the country people.

****

Other works by Ken Wilbur

Blue Eagle:

A story of a young confederate soldier at the end of the Civil War and his black stallion. Their journey from Tennessee to the high plains of the Colorado Territory.

Eagle Brand:

Is the tale of three Colorado men who traveled to Texas and found more than they ever dreamed possible.

Eagle Valley:

Shows that the Native American and the White man could live together in peace – even to the point of helping each other to survive.

Printed in the United States
By Bookmasters